IN PURSUIT OF SPRING

BY

EDWARD THOMAS

THOMAS NELSON AND SONS
LONDON, EDINBURGH, DUBLIN
AND NEW YORK

First Published April 1914

CONTENTS.

LIST OF ILLUSTRATIONS.

From Drawings by Ernest Hazelhurst.

———⋅⋅———

IN PURSUIT OF SPRING.

I.

THIS is the record of a journey from London to the Quantock Hills—to Nether Stowey, Kilve, Crowcombe, and West Bagborough, to the high point where the Taunton-Bridgwater road tops the hills and shows all Exmoor behind, all the Mendips before, and upon the left the sea, and Wales very far off. It was a journey on or with a bicycle. The season was Easter, a March Easter. "A North-Easter, probably?" No. Nor did much north-east go to the making of it. I will give its pedigree briefly, going back only a month— that is, to the days when I began to calculate, or guess methodically, what the weather would be like at Easter.

Perhaps it was rather more than a month before Easter that a false Spring visited London. But I will go back first a little earlier, to one of those great and notable days after the turn of the year that win the heart so, without deceiving it.

The wind blew from the north-west with such peace and energy together as to call up the image of a good giant striding along with superb gestures—like those of a sower sowing. The wind blew and the sun shone over London. A myriad roofs laughed together in the light. The smoke and the flags, yellow and blue and white, waved tumultuously, straining for joy to leave the chimneys and the flagstaffs, like hounds sighting their quarry. The ranges of cloud bathing their lower slopes in the brown mist of the horizon had the majesty of great hills, the coolness and sweetness and whiteness of the foam on the crests of the crystal fountains, and they were burning with light. The clouds did honour to the city, which they encircled as with heavenly ramparts. The stone towers and spires were soft, and luminous as old porcelain. There was no substance to be seen that was not made precious by the strong wind and the light divine. All was newly built to a great idea. The flags were waving to salute the festal opening of the gates in those white walls to a people that should presently surge in and onward to take possession. Princely was to be the life that had this amphitheatre of clouds and palaces for its display.

Of human things, only music—if human it can be called—was fit to match this joyousness and this stateliness. What, I thought, if the pomp of river and roof and cloudy mountain walls of the world be made ready, as so often they had been before, only for the joy of the invisible gods ? For who has not known a day when some notable festival is manifestly celebrated by a most rare nobleness in the ways of the clouds, the colours of the woods, the glitter of the waters, yet on earth all has been as it was wont to be ?

So far, the life of men moving to and fro across the bridges was like the old life that I knew, though, down below, upon the sparkling waters many birds were alighting, or were already seated like wondrous blossoms upon the bulwarks of a barge painted in parrot colours—red and green. When would the entry begin ?

In the streets, for the present, the roar continued of the inhuman masses of humanity, amidst which a child's crying for a toy was an impertinence, a terrible pretty interruption of the violent moving swoon. Between the millions and the one no agreement was visible. The wind summoned the colour in a girl's cheeks. There, one smiled with inward bliss. Another talked serenely with lovely soft mouth and wide eyes that saw only one other pair as the man next her bent his head nearer. The wind wagged the tails of blue or brown fur about the forms of luxurious tall women, and poured wine into their bodies, so that their complexions glowed under their violet hats. But in one moment the passing loveliness of spirit, or form, or gesture, sank and was drowned in the oceanic multitude. A boy had just met his father at a railway station, and was glad; he held the man's hand, and was trotting gently, trying to get him to run—he failed: then in delight put his arm to his father's waist and was carried along thus, half lifted from the ground, for several yards, smiling and chattering like a bird on a waving branch. The two obstructed others, who took a step to left or right in disdain or impatience. Only a child at an alley entrance saw and laughed, wishing she were his sister, and had his father. A moment, and these also were swallowed up.

I came to broader pavements. Here was less haste; and women went in and out of the crowd, not only parallel to the street, but crosswise here and there; and a man could go at any pace, not

of necessity the crowd's. Some of the most beautiful civilized women of the world moved slowly
and musically in an intricate pattern, which any
one could watch freely ; they had a background of
lustrous jewellery, metal-work and glass, gorgeous
cloths and silks, and many had a foil in the stiff
black and white male figures beside them. They
moved without fear. Stately, costly, tender,
beautiful, nevertheless, though so near, they were
seen as in a magic crystal that enshrines the remote and the long dead. They walked as in
dream, regardlessly smiling. They cast their proud
or kind eyes hither and thither. Once in the intense light of a jeweller's shop, spangled with
pearls, diamonds, and gold, a large red hand, cold
and not quite clean, appeared from within, holding
in three fearful, careful fingers a brooch of gold
and diamonds, which it placed among the others,
and then withdrew itself slowly, tremulously, lest
it should work harm to those dazzling cressets.
The eyes of the women watched the brooch : the
red hand need not have been so fearful ; it was
unseen—the soul was hid. Straight through the
women, in the middle of the broad pavement, and
very slowly, went an old man. He was short, and his
patched overcoat fell in a parallelogram from his
shoulders almost to the pavement. From under-

neath his little cap massive gray curls sprouted
and spread over his upturned collar. Just below
the fringe of his coat his bare heels glowed red.
His hands rested deep in his pockets. His face
was almost concealed by curls and collar: all that
showed itself was the glazed cold red of his cheeks
and large, straight nose, and the glitter of gray
eyes that looked neither to left nor to right, but
ahead and somewhat down. Not a sound did he
make, save the flap of rotten leather against feet
which he scarcely raised lest the shoes should fall
off. Doubtless the composer of the harmonies of
this day could have made use of the old man—
doubtless he did; but as it was a feast day of the
gods, not of men, I did not understand. Around
this figure, clad in complete hue of poverty, the
dance of women in violet and black, cinnamon
and green, tawny and gray, scarlet and slate, and
the browns and golden browns of animals' fur, wove
itself fantastically. The dance heeded him not, nor
he the dance. The sun shone bright. The wind
blew and waved the smoke and the flags wildly
against the sky. The horses curved their stout
necks, showing their teeth, trampling, massing
head by head in rank and cluster, a frieze as magnificent as the procession of white clouds gilded,
rolling along the horizon.

That evening, without thought of Spring, I began
to look at my maps.   Spring would come, of course
—nothing, I supposed, could prevent it—and I
should have to make up my mind how to go westward.   Whatever I did, Salisbury Plain was to be
crossed, not of necessity but of choice ; it was, however, hard to decide whether to go reasonably
diagonally in accordance with my western purpose,
or to meander up the Avon, now on one side now
on the other, by one of the parallel river-side roads,
as far as Amesbury.   Having got to Amesbury,
there would be much provocation to continue up
the river among those thatched villages to Upavon
and to Stephen Duck's village, Charlton, and the
Pewsey valley, and so, turning again westward, in
sight of that very tame White Horse above Alton
Priors, to include Urchfont and Devizes.

Or, again, I might follow up the Wylye westward from Salisbury, and have always below me
the river and its hamlets and churches, the wall
of the Plain always above me on the right.   Thus
I should come to Warminster and to the grand
west wall of the Plain which overhangs the town.

The obvious way was to strike north-west over
the Plain from Stapleford up the Winterbourne,
through cornland and sheepland, by Shrewton
and Tilshead, and down again to other waters

at West Lavington.   Or at Shrewton I could turn sharp to the west, and so visit solitary Chitterne and solitary Imber.

I could not decide.   If I went on foot, I could do as I liked on the Plain.   There are green roads leading from everywhere to everywhere.   But, on the other hand, it might be necessary at that time of year to keep walking all day, which would mean at least thirty miles a day, which was more than I was inclined for.   The false Spring, the weather that really deluded me to think it shameful not to trust it, came a month later, and one of its best days was in London.

Many days in London have no weather.   We are aware only that it is hot or cold, dry or wet; that we are in or out of doors; that we are at ease or not.   This was not one of them.   Rain lashed and wind roared in the night, enveloping my room in a turbulent embrace as if it had been a tiny ship in a great sea, instead of one pigeon-hole in a thousand-fold columbarium deep in London. Dawn awakened me with its tranquillity.   The air was sombrely sweet; there was a lucidity under the gloom of the clouds; the air barely heaved with the ebb of storm; and even when the sun was risen it seemed still twilight.   The jangle of the traffic made a wall round about the quiet in which

I lay embedded. I scarcely heard the sound of it; but I could not forget the wall. Within the circle of quiet a parrot sang the street songs of twenty years ago very clearly, over and over again, almost as sweetly as a blackbird. I had heard him many times before, but now he sang differently—I did not know or consider how or why. The song was different as the air was. Yet I could not directly feel the air, because the windows were tightly shut against the soot of four neighbouring chimney-stacks.

Out of doors the business and pleasure of the day kept me a close though a moving prisoner. All the morning and afternoon I was glad to see only one thing that was not a human face. It was a portico of high fluted columns rising in a cliff above an expanse of gravel walks and turf. The gray columns were blackened with soot splashes. The grass and the stone were touched with the sweetness that was in the early air and in the bird's song before the rain had dried and the wind quite departed. Both were blessed with the same pure and lovely union of humid coldness, gloom, and lucidity, so that the portico appeared for a moment to be the entrance to halls of unimagined beauty and holiness, as if I should be admitted through them into the cloud-ramparted city of

2

that earlier day. Nevertheless, I found all inside exactly as it had always been; not only
the expectation but even the memory of what
had fostered it was wiped out without one pause
of disappointment. The sunlight, now and then
flooding and astonishing the interior, fell through
windows that shut out both sky and earth, into an
atmosphere incapable of acknowledging the divinity
of the rays; they were alien, disturbing, hostile.
There was something childish in these displays, so
wasteful and passionate, before the spectacled eyes
of a number of people reading books in the mum-
mied air of a library.

Once more on this February day, at four in the
afternoon, my eyes were unsealed and awakened.
The air in the streets of big dark houses was still
and hazy, but overhead hung the loftiest sky I
had ever seen, and the finest of fine-spun clouds
stretched across the pale blue in long white reefs.
In a few moments I was again under a roof. This
time it was the house of a friend, removed from
busy thoroughfares, very silent within. As the
old country servant, faintly dingy and sinister, led
me up to the usual room, the staircase, and both
the shut and the half-seen apartments on either
hand, were mysterious and depressing, with something massive and yet temporary, as if in a dream

mansion of shadows. Nothing definite was suggested by these doors; anything was possible behind them. Right up to the familiar dark room I always felt the same dull trouble. Then the dim room opened before me: I heard the masterly, kind voice.

It was a high, large room with many corners that I had never explored. The furniture gloomed vaguely above and around the little space that was crossed by our two voices. The long windows were some yards away, and between them and us stood a heavy table, a heavy cabinet, and several chairs. Never had I been to the window and looked out, nor did I to-day. No lamp was lit. We talked, we were silent, and I was content. Now and then I looked towards the window, which framed only the corner of a house near by, the chimneys of farther houses, and a pallor of sky between and above them. I was aware of the slow stealing away of day. I knew it was slow, and twice I looked at a clock to make sure that I was not being deceived. I was aware also of the beauty of this slow fading. No wind moved, nor was any movement anywhere heard or seen. The stillness and silence were great; the tranquillity was even greater: I dipped into it and shared it while I listened and talked. Several times two or three children passed beneath the window and chattered in loud, shrill voices, but they were unseen. Far from disturbing the tranquillity, the sounds were steeped in it; the silence and stillness of the twilight saturated and embalmed them. But pleasant as in themselves they were entirely, they were far more so by reason of what they suggested.

These voices and this tranquillity spoke of Spring. They told me what an evening it was at home. I knew how the first blackbird was whistling in the broad oak, and, farther away—some very far away—many thrushes were singing in the chill, under the pale light fitly reflected by the faces of earliest primroses. The sound of lambs and of a rookery more distant blended in soft roaring. Underfoot everything was soaked—soaked clay, soaked dead grass; and the land was agleam with silver rain pools and channels. I foresaw tempest of rain and wind on the next day. Perhaps imagination of dark, withered, and sodden land, and the change threatening, helped to perfect that sweetness which was not wholly of earth. The songs of the birds were to cease, and, in their place, blackbirds would be clinking nervously in impenetrable thickets long after sundown, when only a narrowing pane of almost lightless light

divided a black mass of cloud from a black horizon.
As in the morning streets the essence of the beauty
was lucidity in the arms of gloom, so it was now
in the clear twilight fields gliding towards black
night, tempest, and perhaps a renewal of Winter. . . .
Then a lamp was carried in.   The children's voices
had gone.   In a little while I rose, and, going out,
saw precisely that long pane of light that I should
have seen low in the west, had I been standing
fifty miles off, looking towards Winchester.

Another evening like this one followed.   To the
south and west of me the Downs were spread out
beyond eyesight.   Their flowing and quiet lines
were an invitation, a temptation.   I should have
liked to set forth immediately, to travel day and
night with that flow and quiet until I reached the
nightingale's song, the apple blossom, the perfume
of sunny earth.   But nothing was more impossible.
The next day was sleet.   The most I could do
was to plan so that perhaps I should find myself
travelling in one of those preludes to Summer
which are less false than this one.   The beautiful
Easters I had known came back to me : Easters of
five years, twenty years ago ; early Easters when
the chiffchaff was singing on March 20 in a soft
wind ; later Easters, when Good Friday brought
the swallow, Saturday the cuckoo, Sunday the

nightingale. I did not forget Easters of snow and
of north wind. In the end I decided to trust to
luck—to start on Good Friday on the chance that I
should meet fine weather at once or in a day or two.
I would go out in that safe, tame fashion, looking
for Spring. The date of Easter made nightingales
and cuckoos improbable ; but I might hope for
the chiffchaff, an early martin, some stitchwort
blossoms, cuckoo flowers, some larch green, some
blackthorn white. I began to think of what the
days would be like. Would there be an invisible
sky and a coldish wind, yet some ground for hoping, because the blackbirds would be content in
their singing at evening, and the dead leaves that
trundle in the road would have decreased to a
handful ? Perhaps there would be another of these
dimly promising days. On the third, would the
misty morning clear slowly, the Downs barely
visible under the low drift, behind which the sky is
caked in cloud, with a dirty silver light from the
interstices ? And would there be one place in this
sky which it would be impossible to gaze at, and
would this at last become dazzling, would the drift
vanish, and the Downs and half the valley be hid
in the foundations of a stationary mass of sunlit
white cloud ? Would the earth begin to crumble
in the warm breeze ? Would the bees be heard

instead of the wind? Would the jackdaws play
and cry far up in the pale vault? Would the low
east become a region of cumulus clouds, old-ivory-
coloured, receding with sunny edges one behind
the other infinitely? Would the evening sky be
downy-white and clouded softly over the dark
copses and the many songs interwoven at seven?
Would a clear still night follow, with Lyra and a
multitude of stars? So I questioned. But I will
relate something of what happened in the month
of waiting and preparation.

Next day the north-east wind began to prevail,
making a noise as if the earth were hollow and
rumbling all through the bright night, and all day a
rhythmless and steady roar. The earth was being
scoured like a pot. If snow fell, there was no
more of it in the valleys than if a white bird had
been plucked by a sparrow-hawk : on the hills it
lasted longer, but as thin as rice the day after
a wedding. The wind was eager enough to scour
me. Doubtless, an old man or two, and an infant
or two, it both scoured and killed. The yellow
celandine flowers were bright but shrivelled; the
ivy gleamed blackly on the banks beside the white
roads. These were days of great rather than
of little things; the north-east wind that was
cleaning, and the world that was being cleaned.

The old man, the child, and the celandine, mattered little. Such days are good to live in, better to remember.

Very meekly, and in the night, the north-east wind gave up its power to the south. Mild, sweet, and soft days followed, when the earth was an invalid certain of recovery, with many delicate smiles and languors and fatigues, and little vain fears or recollections. By St. David's Day violets began to disclose themselves to children and some lovers. . . . Copses, hedges, roadsides, and brooksides were taken possession of by millions of primroses in thick, long-stemmed clusters; their green, only just flowerlike, scent was suited perfectly to the invalid but strengthening earth.

Then for most of a day it rained, and what was done under cover of that deliberate, irresistible rain, only a poet can tell. There are more trees than men on the earth, more flowers than children, and on that day the earth was such as I can imagine it before man or god had been invented. It was an earlier than prehistoric day. The sun rose glimmeringly in mist, as yet not strongly, but sure of victory over chaos. What will happen? What shall come of it? What will be the new thing? On such a day the song of birds was first heard upon the earth. . . . As I went along I found myself repeating with an inexplicable and novel fervour the words, " Glory be to the Father, and to the Son, and to the Holy Ghost, as it was in the beginning, is now, and ever shall be, world without end, Amen." No possible supplication to " Earth, Ocean, Air—Eternal Brotherhood," could have been more satisfying. From time to time other incantations also seemed appropriate, as, for example,—

> " Oh, Santiana's won the day—
> Away, Santiana !—
> Santiana's won the day
> Along the plains of Mexico."

There followed an ordinary fine day, warm but fresh, with more than one light shower out of the south-west during the afternoon; after that a cloudy, rainless day, which people did not call fine, though the chaffinches and thrushes enjoyed it wholly; and after that, rain again, and the elms standing about like conspirators in the mist of the rain, preparing something; then a day, warm and bright, of a heavenly and yet also a spirited loveliness—the best day of the year, when the larks' notes were far beyond counting; and after that wind and rain again; a day of great wind and no rain; then two days of mild, quick air, both glooming into black nights of tumult, with frosty, penitent-looking dawns. Snow succeeded, darkening the air, whitening the sky, on the wings of a strong wind from the north of northwest, for a minute only, but again and again, until by five o'clock the sky was all blue except at the horizon, where stood a cluster of white mountains, massive and almost motionless, in the south above the Downs, and round about them some dusky fragments not fit to be used in the composition of such mountains. They looked as if they were going to last for ever. Yet by six o'clock the horizon was dim, and the clouds all but passed away, the Downs clear and extended; the blackbird singing as if the world were his nest, the wind cold and light, but dying utterly to make way for a beautiful evening of one star and many owls hooting:

The next day was the missel-thrush's and the north-west wind's. The missel-thrush sat well up in a beech at the wood edge and hailed the rain with his rolling, brief song: so rapidly and oft was it repeated that it was almost one long, continuous song. But as the wind snatched away the notes again and again, or the bird changed his perch, or another answered him or took his place, the music was roving like a hunter's. . . . I looked at my maps. Should I go through Swin-

don, or Andover, or Winchester, or Southampton?
I had a mind to compass all four; but the objection was that the kinks thus to be made would
destroy any feeling of advance in the journey. . . .

The night was wild, and on the morrow the earth
lay sleeping a sweet, quiet sleep of recovery from
the wind's rage. The robin could be heard as
often as the missel-thrush. The sleep lasted
through a morning of frost and haze into a clear
day, gentle but bright, and another and another of
cloudy brightness, brightened cloudiness, rounded
off between half-past five and half-past six by
blackbirds singing. The nights were strange children for such days, nights of frantic wind and rain,
threatening to undo all the sweet work in a swift,
howling revolution. Trees were thrown down,
branches broken, but the buds remained.

The north wind made an invasion with horizontal
arrows of pricking hail in the day, and twice in the
night a blue lightning, that long stood brandished
within the room until thunder fell, disembowelling
the universe, with no rolling sound, but a single
plunge and rebound as of an enormous weight.
With the day came snow, hail, and rain, each im-
potent to silence the larks for one minute after it
had ceased. The half-moon at the zenith of a serene,
frosty night led in a morning of mist that filled up

all the hollows of the valley as with snow : each current of smoke from locomotive or cottage lay in solid and enduring vertebræ above the mist : the sun shone upon black rooks cawing moodily, upon snow and freshest green intermingled : the larks soared into the light white cloud; the bullfinch whispered a sweet, cracked melody, almost hid now in hawthorn leaves.

These things in their turn availed nothing against a wind swooping violently all night, sometimes with rain, sometimes without. Neither west wind nor rain respected daybreak : only at half-past one could the sun put his head out to see if the two had done quarrelling with the earth or with one another. The rain gave up, and the loose clouds strewn over the sky had no more order than the linen which was now hurriedly spread on the blossoming gorse-bushes to flatter the sun. In response, the sun poured out light on flooded waters, on purple brook-side thickets of alder, and celandines under them, and on solitary greening chestnuts, as if all was now to be well. The clouds massed themselves together in larger and whiter continents, the blue spaces widened. Yet though the sun went down in peace, what of the morrow ?

Whatever happened, I was to start on Good Friday. I was now deciding that I would go through Salisbury, and over the Plain to West Lavington, and thence either through Devizes or through Trowbridge and Bradford. Salisbury was to be reached by Guildford, Farnham, Alton, Alresford, but perhaps not Winchester—for I could follow down the Itchen to King's Worthy, and then cross those twenty miles of railwayless country by way of Stockbridge, visiting thus Hazlitt's Winterslow. To Guildford there were several possible ways. The ordinary Portsmouth road, smooth enough for roller-skating, and passing through unenclosed piny and ferny commons one after another, did not overmuch attract me. Also, I wanted to see Ewell again, and Epsom, and Leatherhead, and to turn round between hill and water under Leatherhead Church and Mickleham Church to Dorking. Thus my ways out of London were reduced. I could, of course, reach Ewell by way of Kingston, Surbiton, and Tolworth, traversing some of Jefferies' second country, and crossing the home of his " London trout." But this was too much of a digression for the first day.

At any rate the Quantocks were to be my goal. I had a wish of a mildly imperative nature that Spring would be arriving among the Quantocks at the same time as myself—that " the one red leaf the last of its clan," that danced on March 7, 1798, would have danced itself into the grave : that since my journey was to be in " a month before the month of May," Spring would come fast, not slowly, up that way.   Yes, I would see Nether Stowey, the native soil of " Kubla Khan," " Christabel," and " The Ancient Mariner," where Coleridge fed on honey-dew and drank the milk of Paradise.

If I was to get beyond the Quantocks, it would only be for the sake of looking at Taunton or Minehead or Exmoor. Those hills were a distinct and sufficient goal, because they form the boundary between the south-west and the west. Beyond them lie Exmoor, Dartmoor, the Bodmin Moor, and Land's End, a rocky and wilder land, though with many a delicate or bounteous interspace. On this side is the main tract of the south and the south-west, and the Quantocks themselves are the last great strongholds of that sweetness. Thither I planned to go, under the North Downs to Guildford, along the Hog's Back to Farnham, down the Itchen towards Winchester, over the high lands of the Test to Salisbury ; across the Plain to Bradford, over the Mendips to Shepton Mallet, and then under the Mendips to Wells and Glastonbury, along the ridge of the Polden Hills to Bridgwater, and so up to the Quantocks and down to the sea.

I was to start on roads leading into the Epsom

road. Some regret I felt that I could not contrive
to leave by the Brighton road. For I should thus
again have enjoyed passing the green dome of
Streatham Common, the rookery at Norbury, the
goose-pond by the "Wheatsheaf" and "Horse-
shoe," and threading the unbroken lines of Croydon
shops until Haling Park begins on the right hand,
opposite the "Red Deer." The long, low, green
slope of the Park, the rookery elms on it, the chestnuts above the roadside fence, are among the pleasantest things which the besieging streets have made
pleasanter. Haling Down, a straight-ridged and
treeless long hill parallel to the road, is a continuation
of that slope. In the midst it is broken by a huge
chalk-pit, bushy and weathered, and its whole length
is carved by an old road, always clearly marked
either by the bare chalk of its banks or the stout
thorn-bushes attending its course. Blocks of shops
between the grass and the road, a street or two
running up into it, as at the chalk-pit, and the an-
nouncement of building sites, have not spoiled this
little Down, which London has virtually imprisoned. Anywhere in the chalk country its distinct
individuality, the long, straight ridge and even
flank, would gain it honour, but here it is a pure
pastoral. It is good enough to create a poem at
least equal (in everything but length) to "Windsor

Forest " or " Cooper's Hill," if we had a local poet
to-day. Beyond it, enclosed by the Eastbourne
and Brighton roads, is a perfect small region of low
downs, some bare, some wooded, some bushy, having Coulsdon in the centre. . . . But that was not
to be my way.

Next day new dust was blowing over still wet
mud, but the stainless blue of eight o'clock was
veiled at nine. A thin gleam now and then illuminated the oaks, the fagots piled among primroses,
and the copser himself. Half leaning against an
oak, half reclining on his bed between two hurdles,
he smoked and saw steadily and whole the train
that rushed past the wood's edge, the immense white
cloud that pushed up slowly above the horizon,
and the man following the roller down stripe after
stripe of. the next meadow, his head bent, his hand
in his pocket. What sun there was, and perhaps
more, had entered the rook's cawing and the passages from " Madame Angot " tripping out of the
barrel-organ. One isolated bent larch in a dark
wood was green all over, a spirit of acrid green
challenging the darkness. An angry little shower
made my hope sputter, but the gleam—while the
rain, white with light, was still falling—the soft
bright gleam with which the worn flagstones
answered the returning sun seemed to me pure

Spring. If the rain fell again soon afterwards it only enriched the deep, after-rainy blue of evening, and made whiter the one planet that shone at half-past six upon the mud, the straight lines of traffic, and the parallels of white and yellow lamps. As deeply as one pearl dropped in mid-Atlantic was that planet lost in the storms of the night, when the rain and the south-west wind raved together. Yet I had planned to start on the next day.

II.

I HAD planned to start on March 21, and rather late than early, to give the road time for drying. The light arrived bravely and innocently enough at sunrise; too bravely, for by eight o'clock it was already abashed by a shower. There could be no doubt that either I must wait for a better day, or at the next convenient fine interval I must pretend to be deceived and set out prepared for all things. So at ten I started, with maps and sufficient clothes to replace what my waterproof could not protect from rain.

The suburban by-streets already looked rideable; but they were false prophets: the main roads were very different. For example, the surface between the west end of Nightingale Lane and the top of Burntwood Lane was fit only for fancy cycling—in and out among a thousand lakes a yard wide and three inches deep. These should either have been stocked with gold-fish and aquatic plants or drained, but some time had been allowed to pass without either course being adopted. It may be that all the draining forces of the neighbourhood had been directed to emptying the ornamental pond on Wandsworth Common. Empty it was, and the sodden bed did not improve the look of the common—flat by nature, flatter by recent art. The gorse was in bloom amidst a patchwork of turf, gravel, and puddle. Terriers raced about or trifled. A flock of starlings bathed together in a puddle until scared by the dogs. A tall, stern, bald man without a hat strode earnestly in a straight line across the grass and water, as if pleasure had become a duty. He was alone on the common. In all the other residences, that form walls round the common almost on every side, hot-cross buns had proved more alluring than the rain and the south-west wind. The scene was, in fact, one more likely to be pleasing in a picture than in itself. It was tame : it was at once artificial and artless, and touched with beauty only by the strong wind and by the subdued brightness due to the rain. Its breadth and variety were sufficient for it to respond—something as Exmoor or Mousehold Heath or Cefn Bryn in Gower would have responded—to the cloudily shattered light, the threats and the deceptions, and the great sweep of the wind. But there was no one painting those cold expanses of not quite lusty grass, the hard, dull gravel, the shining puddles, the dark gold-flecked gorse, the stiff, scanty trees with black bark and sharp green buds, the comparatively venerable elms of Bolingbroke Grove, the backs and fronts of houses of no value save to their owners, and the tall chimney-stacks northwards. Perhaps only a solitary artist, or some coldish sort of gnome or angel, could have thoroughly enjoyed this moment. That it was waiting for such a one I am certain; I am almost equally certain that he could create a vogue in scenes like this one, which are only about a thousandth part as unpleasant as a cold bath, and possess, furthermore, elements of divinity lacking both to the cold bath and to the ensuing bun.

It is easier to like the blackbird's shrubbery, the lawn, the big elm, or oak, and the few dozen fruit trees, of the one or two larger and older houses surviving—for example, at the top of Burntwood Lane. The almond, the mulberry, the apple trees in these gardens have a menaced or actually caged loveliness, as of a creature detained from some world far from ours, if they are not, as in some cases they are, the lost angels of ruined paradises.

Burntwood Lane, leading down from a residential district to an industrial district, is no longer as pretty as its name. Also, when it seems to be aiming at the country, it turns into a street of maisonettes, with a vista of houses terminated by the two tall red chimneys of the Wimbledon Electricity Works. But it has its character. The Lunatic Asylum helps it with broad, cultivated squares, elms, and rooks' nests, and the voices of cows and pigs behind the railings that line it on the left hand from top to bottom. On the right, playfields waiting to be built all over give it a lesser advantage. How sorry are the unprotected elms on that side ! They will never be old. Man, child, and dog, walking in and out of them, climbing them, kicking and cutting them, have made them as little like trees as it is possible for them to be while they yet live. They have one hour of prettiness, when the leaf-buds are as big as peas on the little side sprays low down. Then on a Saturday —or on a Sunday, when the path is darkened by adults in their best clothes—the children come and pick the sprays in bunches instead of primroses. For there are no primroses, no celandines, no dandelions outside the fences in Burntwood Lane. And Garratt Green at the bottom is now but a railed-in, perfectly level square for games, with rules on a notice-board. It is greener than when it was crossed diagonally by paths, and honoured

on a Saturday by gypsies and coconut-shies.
Probably it now gives some satisfaction to the
greatest number possible, but nobody will ever
again, until After London, think of Garratt Green
as a sort of country place. I went round it and
its footballers in haste. Nor is that thickening
portion of London beyond it easily made to appear beautiful or interesting. It is flat and low,
suitable rather for vegetables than men, and built
on chiefly because people can always be enticed into
new houses. The flatter and lower and more suitable for vegetables, the more easily satisfied are the
people with their houses, partly because they are
poor, partly because they are half country folk and
like this kind of land, it may be, and the river
Wandel, the watercress beds, the swampy places,
the market gardens, the cabbages and lavender,
and Mitcham Fair, more than they would like the
church-parade along Bolingbroke Grove, the bands,
the teetotallers, the atheists, and the tennis-players,
on the commons which have a gravel soil.

As I left the Green I noticed Huntspill Road.
Why is it Huntspill Road ? I thought at once of
Huntspill in Somerset, of Highbridge on the Brue,
of Brent Knoll, of Burnham and Hunt's Pond,
and the sandhills and the clouded-yellow butterflies that shared the hollows of the sandhills with

me in the Summer once. Such is the way of street names, particularly in London suburbs, where free play is given to memory and fancy. I suppose, if I were to look, I should find names as homely as the Florrie Place and Lily Place at lower Farringdon near Alton, or the Susannah's Cottage and Katie's Cottage near Canute's Palace at Southampton. But Beatrice, Ayacanora, or Megalostrate would be as likely. To the casual, curious man, these street names compose an outdoor museum as rich as any in the world. They are the elements of a puzzle map of England which gradually we fill in, now recognizing from a bustop the name of a Wiltshire village, and again among the Downs coming upon a place which had formerly been but a name near Clapham Junction.

Not far beyond Huntspill Road, at what is called (I think) New Wimbledon, I noticed a De Burgh Street. Do you remember how Borrow, speaking of the tricks of fortune, says that he has seen a descendant of the De Burghs who wore the falcon mending kettles in a dingle? He counted himself one of the De Burghs. De Burgh Street is a double row of more than dingy—better than dingy—swarthy, mulatto cottages, ending in a barrier of elm trees. The monotony of the tiny front gardens is broken by a dark pine tree in one, and by an inn called the " Sultan "—not " Sweet Sultan," which is a flower, but " Sultan," a dusky king. And out of the " Sultan," towards me, strode a gaunt, dusky man, with long black ringlets dangling from under his hard hat down over his green and scarlet neckerchief. His tight trousers, his brisk gait, and his hairless jib, were those of a man used to horses and to buyers and sellers of horses. He came rapidly and to beg. Rapid was his begging, exquisitely finished in its mechanical servility. His people were somewhere not far off, said he. That night he had travelled from St. Albans to rejoin them. They were not here : they must be at Wandsworth, with the vans and horses. All questions were answered instantly, briefly, and impersonally. The incident was but a pause in his rapid career from the " Sultan " to Wandsworth. He took the price of a pint with a slight appearance of gratitude, and departed with long, very quick steps, head down, face almost hidden by his bowler.

But there was much to be seen, between Huntspill Road and De Burgh Road. The scene, for instance, from the corner by the " Plough," the " Prince Albert," and the " White Lion," at Summerstown, was curious and typical. These three great houses stand at the edge of the still culti-

vated and unpopulated portion of the flat land
of the Wandel—the allotment gardens, the watercress beds, the meadows plentifully adorned with
advertisements and thinly sprinkled with horse
and cow, but not lacking a rustic house and a
shed or two, and to-day a show of plum-blossom.
This suburban landscape had not the grace of
Haling Park and Down, but at that moment its
best hour was beginning. The main part visible
was twenty acres of damp meadow. On the left
it was bounded by the irregular low buildings of a
laundry, a file and tool factory, and a chamois-
leather mill; on the right by the dirty backs of
Summerstown. On the far side a neat, white,
oldish house was retiring amid blossoming fruit
trees under the guardianship of several elms, and
the shadow of those two tall red chimneys of the
Electricity Works. On my side the meadow had
a low black fence between it and the road, with
the addition, in one place, of high advertisement
boards, behind which lurked three gypsy vans.
A mixture of the sordid and the delicate in the
whole was unmistakable.

Skirting the meadow, my road led up to the
Wandel and a mean bridge. The river here is
broadened for a hundred yards, between the bridge
and the chamois-leather mill or Copper Mill. The

buildings extend across and along one side of the
water ; a meadow comes to the sedgy side opposite. The mill looks old, has tarred boards where
it might have had corrugated iron, and its neighbours are elms and the two chimneys. It is
approached at one side by a lane called Copper Mill
Lane, where the mud is of a sort clearly denoting
a town edge or a coal district. Above the bridge
the back-yards of new houses have only a narrow
waste between them and the Wandel, and on this
was being set up the coconut-shy that would have
been on Garratt Green twenty years ago.

The rain returned as I was crossing the railway
bridge by Haydon's Road station. It was raining
hard when the gypsy left the "Sultan," and still
harder when I turned to the right along Merton
Road. 'Rather than be soaked thus early, I took
the shelter offered by a bird-shop on the left hand.
This was not a cheerful or a pretty place. Overhead hung a row of cages containing chaffinches—
battered ones at a shilling, a neater one at eighteen-
pence—that sang every now and then,—

"My life and soul, as if he were a Greek."

Inside the shop, linnets at half a crown were rushing ceaselessly against the bars of six-inch cages,
their bosoms ruffled and bloody as if from the

strife, themselves like wild hearts beating in breasts too narrow. " House-moulted " goldfinches (price 5s. 6d.) were making sounds which I should have recognized as the twittering of goldfinches had I heard them among thistles on the Down tops. Little, bright foreign birds, that would have been hardly more at home there than here, looked more contented. A gold-fish, six inches long, squirmed about a globe with a diameter of six inches, in the most complete exile imaginable. The birds at least breathed air not parted entirely from the south-west wind which was now soaking the street; but the fish was in a living grave. The place was perhaps more cheerless to look at than to live in, but in a short time three more persons took shelter by it, and after glancing at the birds, stood looking out at the rain, at the dull street, the tobacconist's, news-agent's, and confectioner's shops alone being unshuttered. Presently one of the three shelterers entered the bird-shop, which I had supposed shut; the proprietor came out for a chaffinch; and in a minute or two the customer left with an uncomfortable air and something fluttering in a paper bag such as would hold a penn'orth of sweets. He mounted a bicycle, and I after him, for the rain had forgotten to fall. He turned up to the left towards Morden station, which was my way also. Not far up the road he was apparently unable to bear the fluttering in the paper bag any longer; he got down, and with an awkward air, as if he knew how many great men had done it before, released the flutterer. A dingy cock chaffinch flew off among the lilacs of a garden, saying " Chink." The deliverer was up and away again.

For some distance yet the land was level. The only hill was made by the necessity of crossing a railway at Morden station. At that point rows of houses were discontinued; shops and public-houses with a lot of plate-glass had already ceased. The open stretches were wider and wider, of dark earth, of vegetables in squares, or florists' plantations, divided by hedges low and few, or by lines of tall elm trees or Lombardy poplars. Not quite rustic men and women stooped or moved to and fro among the vegetables: carts were waiting under the elms. A new house, a gasometer, an old house and its trees, lay on the farther side of the big field: behind them the Crystal Palace. On my right, in the opposite direction, the trees massed themselves together into one wood.

It is so easy to make this flat land sordid. The roads, hedges, and fences on it have hardly a reason for being anything but straight. More and more the kind of estate disappears that might

preserve trees and various wasteful and pretty
things : it is replaced by small villas and market
gardens. If any waste be left under the new
order, it will be used for conspicuously depositing
rubbish. Little or no wildness of form or ar-
rangement can survive, and with no wildness a
landscape cannot be beautiful. Barbed wire and
ugly and cruel fences, used against the large and
irresponsible population of townsmen, add to the
charmless artificiality. It was a relief to see a boy
stealing up one of the hedges, looking for birds'
nests. And then close up against this eager agri-
culture and its barbed wires are the hotels, inns,
tea-shops, and cottages with ginger-beer for the
townsman who is looking for country of a more
easy-going nature. This was inhospitable. On
many a fence and gate had been newly written up
in chalk by some prophet: " Eternity," " Believe,"
" Come unto Me."

I welcomed the fences for the sake of what lay
behind them. Now it was a shrubbery, now a
copse, and perhaps a rookery, or a field running
up mysteriously to the curved edge of a wood, and
at Morden Hall it was a herd of deer among the
trees. The hedges were good in themselves, and
for the lush grass, the cuckoo-pint, goose-grass,
and celandine upon their banks. Walking up all

the slightest hills because of the south-west wind, I
could see everything, from the celandines one by
one and the crowding new chestnut leaves, to the
genial red brick tower of St. Laurence's Church
at Morden and the inns one after another—the
"George," the "Lord Nelson," the "Organ," the
"Brick Kiln," the "Victoria." Nelson's hatchment
is still on the wall of Merton Church: his name
is the principal one for inns in the neighbourhood. Ewell, for example, has a "Lord Nelson,"
where the signboard shows Nelson and the tele-
scope on one side, and the *Victory* on the other.

The liberator of the chaffinch and I no longer
had the road to ourselves as we struggled on in
the mud between old houses, villas, dingy tea-
shops, hoardings, and fields that seemed to produce crops of old iron and broken crockery. If
the distant view at one moment was all elm trees,
at the next it was a grand new instalment of London, ten fields away. But all of us must have
looked mainly at the road ahead, making for some
conjectural " world far from ours." The important
thing was to get out of this particular evil, not to
inquire whether worse came after.

Only the most determined, people were on the
road. Motor cycles and side-cars bore middle-
aged men with their wives or children, poorish-

ooking young men with their girls. Once or twice a man dashed by with a pretty girl smiling above his back wheel, perfectly balanced. But the greater number of my fellow-travellers were cyclists carrying luncheons and waterproofs. In one band seven or eight lean young chaps in dark clothes bent over their handle-bars, talking in jerks as they laboured, all stopping together at any call for a drink or to mend a puncture. They swore furiously, but (I believe) not in anger, at a nervous woman crossing in front of them. If conversation flagged, one or other of them was certain to break out into song with,—

> " Who were you with last night
> Out in the pale moonlight ?
> It wasn't your missus,
> It wasn't your ma.
> Ah, ah, ah, ah ! . . . ah !
> Will you tell your missus
> When you get home
> Who you were with last night ? "

The clouds hung like pudding-bags all over the sky, but the sad, amorous, jaunty drivel seemed to console them.

Some way past Morden these braves were jeering at the liberator of the chaffinch, who stood in the middle of the road with a book and pencil. He was drawing a weather-vane above a house on the left hand. The long, gilt dragon, its open mouth, sharp ears, sharp upright wings, and thin curled tail, had attracted him, although the arrow-head at the tip of the tail was pointing south-westward, and rain was falling. " It's rather curious," he remarked, as I came up to him, " there is no ingenuity in weather-vanes. One has to put up with the Ship and the Cock erected over the Imperial Hotel in Russell Square, and think oneself really lucky to come across the Centaur with his bow and arrow at the brass-foundry, you know, on the left just before you come to the top of Tottenham Court Road from Portland Road station." But it was blowing hard, and there was little reason for me to suppose that he was addressing me, or for him to suppose that I heard him. However, it was a kind of introduction. On we rode.

I had been about two hours reaching the gate of Nonsuch Park, and the fountain and cross there commemorating a former mistress, Charlotte Farmer, who died in 1906. The other man was reading aloud the inscription,—

> " As thirsty travellers in a desert land
>   Welcome a spring amidst a waste of sand,
>   So did her kindly actions cheer the sad,
>   Refresh the worn, and make the weary glad."

I tried to get water, but there was none. Nevertheless, the fountain was a pretty thing on that plot of grass where the road zigzags opposite the gate and avenue of Nonsuch. A dove and an olive branch, of ruddiest gilding, is perched on the cross tip.

" Wretched weather," said the man, speaking through the pencil in his mouth, as he straddled on to his bicycle. At Ewell I lost him by going round behind the new church to look at the old tower. This completely ivy-covered square tower is all that remains of an old church. If the rest was as little decayed, there can hardly have been a good reason for demolishing it. The doors were locked. I could only walk about among the trees, glancing at the tombs of the Glyn family, and the headstone of Edward Wells (who died in 1742, at the age of sixteen) and the winged skull adorning it.

Ewell was the first place on my road which bore a considerable resemblance to a country town. It stands at the forking of a Brighton and a Worthing road. Hereby rises the Hogsmill river; its water flows alongside the street, giving its name to the " Spring Inn." The name Ewell, like that of Oxfordshire Ewelme, seems and is said to be connected with the presence of water. The place is not a mere roadside collection of houses with a variegated, old look, but a town at which roads meet, pause, take a turn or two, and exchange greetings,

4

before separating from one another and from Ewell. The town probably struck those escaping Londoners on bicycles as one where the sign of the " Green Man " was in keeping. Comfortable houses on the outskirts, with high trees and shrubberies, and an avenue of limes crossing the road at right angles, confirm the fancy. It marked a definite stage on the road from London.

The end of Ewell touched the beginning of Epsom, which had to be entered between high walls of advertisements—yards of pictures and large letters—asserting the virtues of clothes, food, drugs, etc., one sheet, for example, showing that by eating or drinking something you gained health, appetite, vigour, and a fig-leaf. The exit was better.

Epsom had the same general effect as Ewell, but more definite and complete, thanks to a few hundred yards of street broad enough for a market which, for the most part, satisfied the town eye as coun- trified and old-fashioned. Over one of its corn- chandlers' a carved horse's head was stuck up. There was an empty inn called the " Tun," a restaurant named after Nell Gwynn. True, there is a fortnight's racing yearly, and a number of railway stations, in consequence ; and " Lord Arthur Savile's Crime " is on sale there : but, as in Nell Gwynn's time and Defoe's time, it is a place for putting off London thoughts. There is no king there now, no king's mistress presumably, no nightly ball even in July, no bowls, no strutting to the Wells to drink what the chemist sells at two-pence a pound, no line of trees down the middle of the broad street. Nor, accordingly, is there the same wintry dereliction as in those days. When the leaves fall in Autumn the people do not all fly, the houses are not all shut up, the walks do not go out of repair, the roads do not become full of sloughs. But it always was a pleasure resort. For more than a hundred years before railways, London business men used to keep their families at Epsom and ride daily to and from the Exchange or their warehouses. The very market that it had on Fridays had been obtained for it by a plotting apothecary named Livingstone. This man tried to diddle the world by putting up a pump, not over the good old cathartic spring, but over a new one that was not cathartic; and the world gave up both old and new. To-day only the poor and simple go to Epsom for pleasure apart from racing. Anybody and everybody with feet or wheels can get there from London on a holiday or even a half-holiday.

The exit from Epsom was almost free from advertisements. And then the common: it had a sea-like breadth and clearness. The one man

among the soaked, flowering gorse-bushes and new
green hawthorn was extremely like the liberator
of the chaffinch and collector of weather-vanes.
He was sketching something in the rain. The only
others of humankind visible were on the road,
struggling south-west or rushing towards London,
or on the side of the road, hoping to sell ginger-beer
and lemonade to travellers. This hedgeless gorse-
land, first on both sides, then on the right only,
reached to the verge of Ashtead, but with some
change of character. The larger part was gently
billowing gorse flower and hawthorn leaf. The
last part was flat, wet, and rushy. The gorse came
to an end, and here was a copse of oak. At intervals of thirty yards or so were oaks as old as Epsom,
of a broad kind, forking close to the ground, iron-
coloured and stained with faint green. Oaks not
more than forty or fifty years old, tall instead of
spreading, their lower branches broken off, grew
between. Among these, dead fern and bramble
with its old leaves made distinct island thickets, out
of which stood a few thorns. And the thin grasses
around the thickets were strewn with dead twigs
and leaves, and some paper and broken bottles left
there in better weather. A robin sang in one of
the broad oaks, whether any one listened or not.

On the opposite side of the road—that is to say,

on the left—the common had given way to Ashtead
Park.   There the big iron-coloured oaks stood
aristocratically about on gentle green slopes.   To
Ashtead Park belonged the Hon. Mary Greville
Howard, who died in 1877, at the age of ninety-two,
and is commemorated by a fountain on the right
hand which gave me this information.   The fountain
is placed on a square of much-trodden bare earth
close to the road, surmounted by a cross.   Whatever
were the good deeds which persuaded her friends
to erect the fountain, that was a good deed.   It was
not dry, and, I have been told, never is.

Ashtead itself is more suburban than either Ewell
or Epsom.   It appeared to be a collection of residences
about as incapable of self-support as could anywhere
be found—a private-looking, respectable, inhospitable place that made the rain colder, and doubtless,
in turn, coloured the spectacles it was seen through.
The name of its inn, the "Leg of Mutton and
Cauliflower," may be venerable, but it smacked of
suburban fancy, as if it had been bestowed to
catch the pennies of easy-going lovers of quaintness.

They were beginning to create a new Ashtead a
little farther on.   A placard by a larch copse at the
edge of a high-walled marl-pit, announced that
convenient and commanding houses were to be
built shortly to supply the new golf links with

golfers. A road had been driven through the estate. The young, green larches stood at the entrance like well-drilled liveried pages, ready to give way or die according to the requirements of golfers, but for the present enjoying the rain and looking as larch-like as possible above the curved gray wall of the pit.

Not much after this, Leatherhead began, two broken lines of villas, trees, and shrubberies, leading to a steep country street and, at its foot, the Mole,

> " Four streams: whose whole delight in island lawns,
> Dark-hanging alder dusks and willows pale
> O'er shining gray-green shadowed waterways,
> Makes murmuring haste of exit from the vale—
> Through fourteen arches voluble
> Where river tide-weed sways." . . .

As I looked this time from Leatherhead Bridge, I recalled " Aphrodite at Leatherhead," and these, its opening lines, by John Helston, the town's second poet. It is no new thing to stop on the bridge and look up the river to the railway bridge, and down over the divided water to the level grass, the tossing willows, the tall poplars scattered upon it, the dark elms beside, and Leatherhead rising up from it to the flint tower of St. Mary and St. Nicholas, and its umbrageous churchyard and turf as of grass-green silk. The bridge is good in itself,

and the better for this view and for the poem.
The adjacent inn, the "Running Horse," and
Elinour Rumming who brewed ale there and sold
it to travellers—

> "Tinkers and sweaters and swinkers
> And all good ale-drinkers "—

four hundred years ago, these were the theme of
a poet, Henry the Eighth's laureate, John Skelton.

Having ridden down to the bridge, I walked up
again, for I had no intention of going on over the
Mole by the shortest road to Guildford. It is a good
road, but a high and rather straight one through
parks and cornland, and scarcely a village. The
wide spaces on both hands, and the troops and
clusters of elm trees, are best in fine weather,
particularly in Autumn. I took the road through
Mickleham and Dorking. Thus I wound along,
having wooded hills, Leatherhead Downs, Mickleham Downs, Juniper Hill, and Box Hill, always
steep above on the left, and on the right the Mole
almost continually in sight below.

They were still worshipping in the Church of St.
Mary and St. Nicholas. Outside it what most
pleased me were the cross near a young cedar
which was erected in 1902 " to the praise and
glory of God, and the memory of the nameless
dead," and the epitaph: "Here sleepeth, awaiting

the resurrection of the just, William Lewis, Esq., of the East India Company." The memory of a human being that can exist without a name is but the shadow of the shadow that a name casts, and it is hard not to wonder what effect the cross can have on those who await the resurrection of the just, or indeed, on any one but Geraldine Rickards, at whose expense it was placed here.

The road, bending round under the churchyard and its trees, followed the steeper side of the Mole valley, and displayed to me the meadow, young corn, and ploughland, running up from the farther bank to beech woods. The clouds were higher and harder. The imprisoned pale sun, though it could not be seen, could be felt at the moments when a bend offered shelter from the wind. The change was too late for most of my fellow-travellers : they had stopped or turned back at Leatherhead. I was almost alone as I came into Mickleham, except for a horseman and his dog. This man was a thick, stiff man in clay-coloured rough clothes and a hard hat ; his bandy, begaitered legs curled round the flanks of a piebald pony as thick and stiff as himself. He carried an ash-plant instead of a riding-whip, and in his mouth a pipe of strong, good tobacco. I had not seen such a country figure that day, though I dare say there were many

among the nameless dead in Leatherhead churchyard, awaiting the resurrection of the just with
characteristic patience.   His dog also was clay-
coloured, as shaggy and as large as a sheep, and
exceedingly like a sheep.   Probably he was a man
who could have helped me to understand, for example, the epitaph of Benjamin Rogers in Mickleham churchyard,—

> " Here peaceful sleep the aged and the young,
>   The rich and poor, an undistinguished throng.
>   Time was these ashes lived ; a time must be
>   When others thus shall stand and look at thee."

I had at first written,—

> " Time was these ashes lov'd."

His wife, Mary, who died at fifty-five in 1755, is
hard by under an arch of ancient ivy against the
wall.   She speaks from the tomb,—

> " How lov'd, how valu'd once avails thee not :
>   To whom related, or by whom begot.
>   A heap of dust alone remains of thee.
>   'Tis all thou art, and all the proud shall be."

That this desperate Christian, Mary Rogers, had
any special knowledge of these matters, I have no
reason for believing.   I even doubt if she really
thought that love was of as little importance as
having a lord in the family.   The lines were composed in a drab ecstasy of conventional humility,

lacking genuine satisfaction in the thought that
she and the more beautiful and the better-dressed
were become equals. But I did not ask the clay-
coloured man's opinion. I rode behind him into
Mickleham, and there lost him between the " Running Horse " (or, at least, an inn with two racing
horses for a sign) and the " William the Fourth."
The loyalty of Mickleham, in thus preserving the
memory of a sort of a king for three-quarters of a
century, is sublime. Mickleham is, apart from its
gentlemen's residences, an old-fashioned place, ac-
commodating itself in a picturesque manner to the
hillside against which it has to cling, in order to
avoid rolling into the Mole. The root-suckers and
the trunk shoots of the elm trees were in tiny leaf
beside the road, the horse-chestnuts were in large
but still rumpled leaf. The celandines on the
steep banks found something like sunbeams to
shine in. On the smooth slopes the grass was
perfect, alternating with pale young corn, and with
arable squares where the dung was waiting for a
fine day before being spread. The small flints of
the ploughland were as fresh. and as bright as
flowers.

When I got to Burford Bridge, the only man at
the entrance of the Box Hill footpath was a man
selling fruit and drink and storing bicycles, or

oping to begin doing these things. One motor
ar stood at the hotel door. The hill was bare,
xcept of trees. But it would take centuries to
vipe away the scars of the footpaths up it.
'or it has a history of two hundred years as a
pleasure resort. Ladies and gentlemen used to go
on a Sunday from Epsom to take the air and walk
in the woods. The landlord of the " King's Arms "
at Dorking furnished a vault under a great beech
on top, with chairs, tables, food, and drink. It was
ike a fair, what with the gentry and the country
people crowding to see and to imitate. But the
young men of Dorking were very virtuous in those
days, or were anxious that others should be so.
They paid the vault a visit on a Saturday and blew
it up with gunpowder to put a stop to the Sabbath
merriment. They, at least, did not believe that in
the dust they would be merely the equals of the
frivolous and fresh-air-loving rich.

Dorking nowadays has no objection to the
popularity of Box Hill and similar resorts. It is
a country town not wholly dependent on London,
but its shops and inns are largely for the benefit of
travellers of all degrees, and a large proportion of
its inhabitants were not born in Dorking and will
not die there. A number of visitors were already
streaming back under umbrellas to the railway

stations, for again it rained. The skylarks sang in the rain, but as man was predominant hereabouts, the general impression was cheerless. To many it must have seemed absurd that the Government— say, Mr. Lloyd George—or the County Council, or the Lord Mayor of Dorking, could not arrange for Good Friday to be a fine day. The handfuls of worshippers may have been more content, but they did not look so. Three-quarters of the windows in the long, decent high street were shuttered or blinded. Unless it was some one entering the " Surrey Yeoman " or " White Horse," nobody did anything but walk as rapidly and as straight as possible along the broad flagged pavement.

Only a robust and happy man, or one in love, can be indifferent to this kind of March weather. Only a lover or a poet can enjoy it. The poet naturally thought of here and on such a day was Meredith of Box Hill. This man,

> " Quivering in harmony with the tempest, fierce
> And eager with tempestuous delight,"

was one of the manliest and deepest of earth's lovers who have written books. From first to last he wrote as an inhabitant of this earth, where, as Wordsworth says, " we have our happiness or not at all," just or unjust. Meredith's love of earth was n its ki   as a more

earthly   a quality

almost   Iis earliest

poems v   n and wind.

He pra   and fields "

would r   end of his life

he wrot   poems of age,

the one   y-leaf of Mr.

Hudson's   ...ventures among Birds : "

> " Once I was part of the music I heard
> On the boughs, or sweet between earth and sky,
> For joy of the beating of wings on high
> My heart shot into the breast of a bird.

> " I hear it now and I see it fly,
> And a life in wrinkles again is stirred,
> My heart shoots into the breast of a bird,
> As it will for sheer love till the last long sigh."

What his " Juggling Jerry " said briefly—

> " Yonder came smells of the gorse, so nutty,
> Gold-like, and warm : it's the prime of May.
> Better than mortar, brick, and putty
> Is God's house on a blowing day "—

he himself said at greater length, with variations and footnotes.

Love of earth meant to him more than is commonly meant by love of Nature. Men gained substance and stability by it ; they became strong—

> "Because their love of earth is deep,
>   And they are warriors in accord
>   With life to serve." . . .

In his two sonnets called "The Spirit of Shakespeare" he said,—

> "Thy greatest knew thee, Mother Earth; unsoured
>   He knew thy sons. He probed from hell to hell
>   Of human passions, but of love deflowered
>   His wisdom was not, for he knew thee well.
>   Thence came the honeyed corner at his lips." .   .

Love of earth meant breadth, perspective, and proportion, and therefore humour,—

> "Thunders of laughter, clearing air and heart."

His Melampus, servant of Apollo, had a medicine, a "juice of the woods," which reclaimed men,—

> "That frenzied in some delirious rage
>   Outran the measure." . . .

So, in "The Appeasement of Demeter," it was on being made to laugh that the goddess relented from her devastating sorrow, and the earth could revive and flourish again. The poet's kinship with earth taught him to look at lesser passing things with a smile, yet without disdain; and he saw the stars as no "distant aliens" or "senseless powers," but as having in them the same fire as we ourselves, and could, nevertheless, turn from them to sing "A Stave of Roving Tim :—"

> " The wind is east, the wind is west,
>   Blows in and out of haven ;
> The wind that blows is the wind that's best,
>   And croak, my jolly raven.
> If here awhile we jigged and laughed,
>   The like we will do yonder ;
> For he's the man who masters a craft,
>   And light as a lord can wander.

> " So foot the measure, Roving Tim,
>   And croak, my jolly raven.
> The wind, according to his whim,
>   Is in and out of haven."

The " bile and buskin " attitude of Byron upon
the Alps caused him to condemn " Manfred,"
pronouncing, as one having authority,—

> " The cities, not the mountains, blow
>   Such bladders ; in their shape's confessed
>   An after-dinner's indigest."

For his earth was definitely opposed to the " city."
He cried to the singing thrush in February,—

> " I hear, I would the City heard.

> " The City of the smoky fray ;
>   A prodded ox, it drags and moans ;
>   Its morrow no man's child ; its day
>   A vulture's morsel beaked to bones." . . .

He tried to persuade the city that earth was not
" a mother whom no cry can melt." But his song
was not clear enough, and when it was understood

it said chiefly that man should love battle and
seek it, and so make himself, even if a clerk or a
philosopher, an animal worthy of the great globe,
careless of death :—

> " For love we Earth, then serve we all :
> Her mystic secret then is ours :
> We fall, or view our treasures fall,
> Unclouded, as beholds her flowers
>
> " Earth, from a night of frosty wreck,
> Enrobed in morning's mounted fire,
> When lowly, with a broken neck,
> The crocus lays her cheek to mire."

He advanced farther, fanatically far, when he said
of the lark's song,—

> " Was never voice of ours could say
> Our inmost in the sweetest way,
> Like yonder voice aloft, and link
> All hearers in the song they drink.
> Our wisdom speaks from failing blood,
> Our passion is too full in flood,
> We want the key of his wild note
> Of truthful in a tuneful throat,
> The song seraphically free
> Of taint of personality." . . .

An impossibly noble savage might seem to have
been his desire, a combination of Shakespeare and
a Huron, of a " wild god-ridden courser " and a
study chair, though in practice perhaps a George
Borrow delighted him less than a Leslie Stephen.

But what he thought matters little compared with what he succeeded in saying, and with that sensuousness and vigour, both bodily and intellectual, which at his best he mingled as few poets have done. His " Love in the Valley " is the most English of love poems : the girl and the valley are purely and beautifully English. His early poem, " Daphne," though treating a Greek myth, is equally English— altogether an open-air piece. No pale remembered orb, but the sun itself, and the wind, sweeten and brace the voluptuousness of both poems. And therefore it is that in passing Box Hill, whether the leaves of " the sudden-lighted whitebeam " are flashing, or lying, as now they were, but dimly hoary in the paths, I think of Meredith as I should not think of other poets in their territories. He was not so much an admirer and lover of Nature, like other poets, as a part of her, one of her most splendid creatures, fit to be ranked with the whitebeam, the lark, and the south-west wind that—

> "Comes upon the neck of night,
> Like one that leapt a fiery steed
> Whose keen, black haunches quivering shine
> With eagerness and haste." . . .

Riding against the south-west wind is quite another thing. That fiery steed which I had been dragging with me, as it were, instead of riding it,

5

was not in the least exhausted, and I knew that
I was unlikely to reach Farnham that evening.
The telegraph wires wailed their inhuman lamen-
tation. Thunder issued a threat of some sort
far off.

At three, after eating, I was on the road again,
making for Guildford by way of Wotton, Shere,
and Shalford. If Dorking people will not have
wine and women on top of Box Hill on a Sunday,
they were, at any rate, strolling on the paths of
their roadside common. The road was level, impossible to cycle on against the wind. But the
eye was not starved; there was no haste. I now
had the clear line of the Downs on my right hand,
and was to have them so to Shalford. At first, in
the region of Denbies, they were thoroughly tamed,
their smoothness made park-like, their trees mostly
fir. Beyond, their sides, of an almost uniform
gentle steepness, but advancing and receding,
hollowed and cleft, were adorned by unceasingly
various combinations of beech wood, of scattered
yew and thorn, of bare ploughland or young corn,
and of naked chalk. The rolling commons at their
feet, Milton Heath and Westcott Heath, were
traversed by my road. Milton Heath, except for
some rugged, heathery, pine-crested mounds on the
right, was rather unnoticeable in comparison with

Buryhill, a roof-like hill at right angles to the road
on my left. This hill has a not very high but
distinct, even ridge, and steep slopes of grass. Its
trees are chiefly upon the top, embowering a classic,
open summer-house.

After Milton Street came Westcott Heath and a
low shingled spire up amid the gorse. The road was
now cutting through sand, and the sand walls were
half overgrown with moss and gorse, ivy and celandine, and overhung by wild cherry and beech. Behind me, as I climbed, a moment's sunlight brought
out the white scar of Box Hill.

Between the rising road and the Downs lay a
hollow land, for nearly two miles occupied in its
lowest part by the oaks of a narrow wood, called
Deerleap Wood, running parallel to the road:
sometimes the gray trunks were washed faintly
with light, the accumulated branch-work proved
itself purplish, and here and there the snick of a
lost bough was bright. Over the summit of the
wood I could see the chalky ploughland or pasture
of the Downs, and their beechen ridge. The hollow land has a kind of island, steep and naturally moated, within it, and close to the road.
Here stands Wotton Church, the home of dead
Evelyns of Wotton, alone among tall beeches and
chestnuts.

I had left behind me most cyclists from London, but I was now continually amongst walkers. There were a few genial muscular Christians with their daughters, and equally genial muscular agnostics with no children; bands of scientifically-minded ramblers with knickerbockers, spectacles, and cameras; a trio of young chaps singing their way to a pub.; one or two solitaries going at five miles an hour with or without hats; several of a more sentimental school in pairs, generally chosen from both sexes, disputing as to the comparative merits of Mr. Belloc and Mr. Arthur Sidgwick; and a few country people walking, not for pleasure, but to see friends seven or eight miles away, whom perhaps they had not visited for years, and, after such a Good Friday as this, never will again.

These travellers gave me a feeling that I had been forestalled (to put it mildly), and as the light began to dwindle, and to lose all intention of being brilliant, I allowed Guildford to hover before my mind's eye, particularly when I saw St. Martha's Church, a small, clear hilltop block six miles away, and I knew that Guildford was not two miles from it, by the Pilgrim's Way or not. It was a satisfaction, though a trifling one, to be going with the water which was making for the Wey at Shalford. The streamlet, the Tillingbourne,

began to assert itself at Abinger Hammer. Just
before that village it runs alongside the road instead of a hedge, nourishing willows and supply-
ing the bronzed watercress beds. The beginning
of the village is a wheelwright's shed under an
elm by the road. Many hoops of wheels lean
against the shed, many planks against the elm.
The green follows, and Abinger Hammer is built
round it. I preferred Gomshall—which only showed
to the main road its inns and brewery—and the
wet, bushy Gomshall Common. It is a resort of
gypsies. A van full of newly-made baskets stood
among the bushes, and the men sat on the shafts
instead of joining the ramblers at the " Black
Horse " or the " Compasses." The downs opposite
them were speckled black with yew.

I did not stop at Shere, " the prettiest village in
Surrey," and I saw no reason why it should not
bear the title, or why it should be any the better
liked for it. But I went to see the Silent Pool.
Until it has been seen, everything is in the name.
I had supposed it circular, tenebrous, and deep
enough to be the receptacle of innumerable romantic skeletons. It is, in fact, an oblong pond of
the size of a swimming bath, overhung on its
two long sides and its far, short side, by ash trees.
Its unrippled lymph, on an irregular chalk bottom

of a singular pallid green, was so clear and thin
that it seemed not to be water. It concealed
nothing. A few trout glided here and there over
the chalk or the dark green weed tufts. It had no
need of romantic truth or fiction. Its innocent
lucidity fascinated me.

Now another short cut to Guildford offered itself,
by the road—an open and yellow road—up over
Merrow Down. But the Downs were beginning to
give me some shelter, and I went on under them,
glad of the easier riding. The Tillingbourne here
was running closer under the Downs, and the river
level met the hillside more sharply than before.
The road bent above the meadows and showed them
flat to the very foot of a steep, brown slope covered
with beeches. The sky lightened—lightened too
much : St. Martha's tower, almost reaching up into
the hurrying white rack, was dark on its dark hill.
So I came to Albury, which has the streamlet between it and the Downs, unlike Abinger Hammer,
Gomshall, and Shere. The ground, used for vegetables and plum trees, fell steeply down to the
water, beyond which it rose again as steeply in a
narrow field bounded horizontally by a yet steeper
strip of hazel coppice ; beyond this again the rise
was continued in a broader field extending to the
edge of the main hillside beechwood. Albury is

one of those villages possessing a neglected old church and a brand-new one. In this case the new is a decent enough one of alternating flint and stone, built among trees on a gradual rise. But the old one is too much like a shameless unburied corpse.

Twice I crossed the Tillingbourne, and came to where it broadened into a pond. This water on either side of the road was bordered by plumed sedges and clubbed bulrushes. At the far side, under the wooded Downside crowned by St. Martha's, was a pale, shelterless mill of a ghostly bareness. The aspens were breaking into yellow-green leaves round about, especially one prone aspen on the left where a drain was belching furious, tawny water into the stream, and shaking the spears of the bulrushes.

As I went on towards Chilworth, gorse was blossoming on the banks of the road. Behind the blossom rose up the masses of hillside wood, now scarcely interrupted save by a few interspaces of lawn-like grass; and seated at the foot of all this oak and pine were the Chilworth powder mills. Two centuries have earned them nobody's love or reverence; for there is something inhuman, diabolical, in permitting the union which makes these unrelated elements more powerful than any beast, crueller than any man.

Crossing the little railway from the mills, I came in sight of the Hog's Back, by which I must go to Farnham. That even, straight ridge pointing westward, and commanding the country far away on either side, must have had a road along it since man went upright, and must continue to have one so long as it is a pleasure to move and to use the eyes together. It is a road fit for the herald Mercury and the other gods, because it is as much in heaven as on earth. The road I was on, creeping humbly and crookedly to avoid both the steepness of the hills and the wetness of the valley, was by comparison a mole run. Between me and the Hog's Back flowed the Wey, and as the Tillingbourne approached it the valley spread out and flattened into Shalford's long, wet common. My road crossed the common, a rest for gypsies and their ponies. Shalford village also is on the flat, chiefly on the right hand side of the road, nearer the hill, and away from the river, so that its outlook over the levels gives it a resemblance to a seaside village. Instead of the sea it had formerly a fair ground of a hundred and forty acres. Its inn is the "Queen Victoria"—charmless name.

To avoid the Wey and reach Guildford, which is mainly on this side of the water, I had to turn sharp to the right at Shalford, and to penetrate, along with the river, the hills which I had been following. Within half a mile of Guildford I was at the point where the Pilgrim's Way, travelling the flank of these hills, descends towards the Wey and the Hog's Back opposite. A small but distinct hill, with a precipitous, sandy face, rises sheer out of the far side of the river where the road once crossed. The silver-gray square of the ruins of St. Catherine's Chapel tops the cliff. The river presently came close to my bank; the road climbed to avoid it, and brought me into Guildford by Quarry Road, well above the steep-built, old portion of the town and its church and rookery sycamores, though below the castle.

The closed shops, plate glass, and granite roadway of the High Street put the worst possible appearance on the rain that suddenly poured down at six. A motor car dashed under the "Lion" arch for shelter. The shop doorways were filled by foot-passengers. The plate glass, the granite, and the rain rebounding from it and rushing in two torrents down the steep gutters, made a scene of physical and spiritual chill under a sky that had now lost even the pretence to possess a sun. I had thought not to decide for or against going on to Farnham that night until I had drunk tea. But having once sat in a room—not of the "Jolly

Butcher," but a commercial temperance hotel—
where I could only hear the rain falling from the
sky and dripping from roofs, I glided into the
resolution to spend the night there. A fire was
lit; the servant stood a poker vertically against
the grate to make it burn; and, after some mis-
givings, it did burn. The moon was mounting the
clear east, and Venus stood with Orion in the west
above a low, horizontal ledge of darkest after-sun-
set cloud. There could not have been a better
time for those ten miles to Farnham; but I did
not go. Not until after supper did I go out to
look at the night I had lost, the cold sea of sky,
the large bright moon, the white stars over the
shimmering roofs, and the yellow street lamps and
window panes of Guildford. I walked haphazard,
now to the right, now to the left, often by narrow
passages and dark entries. I skirted the railings
of the gardens which have been made out of the
castle site, the square ivy-patched keep, the dry
moat full of sycamores; and hereby was a kissing
corner. I crossed Quarry Road and went down
Mill Lane to the " Miller's Arms," the water-
works, and the doubled Wey roaring in turbid
streams. A footbridge took me to Mill Mead, the
" Britannia," and the faintly nautical cottages
that look, over a gas-lit paved space, at the river

and the timber sheds of the other bank. The
dark water, the dark houses, the silvered, wet,
moonlit streets, called for some warm, musical life
in contrast. But except that a sacred concert
was proceeding near the market place, there was
nothing like it accessible. Many couples hurried
along: at corners here and there a young man,
or two young men, talked to a girl. The inns were
not full, too many travellers having been discour-
aged. I had the temperance commercial hotel to
myself, but for two men who had walked from
London and had no conversation left in them,
as was my case also. I dallied alternately with
my maps and with the pictures on the wall. One
of these I liked, a big square gloomy canvas, where
a dark huntsman of Byron's time, red-coated and
clean-shaven, turned round on his horse to cheer
the hounds, one of them almost level with him,
glinting pallid through the mist of time, two others
just pushing their noses into the picture; it had a
background of a dim range of hills and a spire.
The whole picture was as dim as memory, but more
powerful to recall the nameless artist and nameless
huntsman than that cross at Leatherhead.

III

GUILDFORD TO DUNBRIDGE.

COCKS crowing and wheels thundering on granite waked me at Guildford soon after six. I was out at seven, after paying 3s. 6d. for supper and bed : breakfast I was to have at Farnham. I have often fared as well as I did that night at a smaller cost, and worse at a larger. At Guildford itself, for example, I went recently into a place of no historic interest or natural beauty, and greenly consented to pay 3s. for a bed, although the woman, in answer to my question, said that the charge for supper and breakfast would be according to what I had. What I had for supper was two herrings and bread and butter, and a cup of coffee afterwards ; for breakfast I had bacon and bread and tea. The supper cost 1s. 6d., exclusive of the coffee ; the breakfast cost 1s. 6d. exclusive of the tea. Nor did these charges prevent the boots, who had not cleaned my boots, from hanging round me at parting, as if I had been his long-lost son.

The beautiful, still, pale morning was as yet clouded by the lightest of white silk streamers. The slates glimmered with yesterday's rain in the rising sun. It was too fine, too still, too sunny, but the castle jackdaws rejoiced in it, crying loudly in the sycamores, on the old walls, or high in air. By the time I was beginning to mount the Hog's Back, clouds not of silk were assembling. They passed away; others appeared, but the rain was not permitted to fall. Many miles of country lay cold and soft, but undimmed, on both hands. On the north it was a mostly level land where hedgerow trees and copses, beyond the first field or two, made one dark wood to the eye, but rising to the still darker heights of Bisley and Chobham on the horizon, and gradually disclosing the red settlements of Aldershot and Farnborough, and the dark high land of Bagshot. On the south at first I could see the broken ridge of Hindhead, Blackdown, and Olderhill, and through the gap a glimpse of the Downs; then later the piny country which culminates in the dome of Crooksbury Hill; and nearer at hand a lower but steeply rising and falling region of gorse, bracken, and heather intermingled with ploughland of almost bracken colour,

and with the first hop gardens. Both the level-
seeming sweep on the north and the hills of the
south, clear as they were in that anxious light,
were subject to the majestic road on the Hog's
Back. A mile out of Guildford the road is well
upon the back, and for five or six miles it runs
straight, yet not too straight, with slight change
of altitude, yet never flat, and for the most part
upon the very ridge—the topmost bristles—of the
Hog's Back. The ridge, in fact, has in some parts
only just breadth enough to carry the road, and
the land sinks away rapidly on both hands, giving
the traveller the sensation of going on the crest of
a stout wall, surveying his immense possessions
northward and southward. The road has a further
advantage that would be great whatever its position, but on this ridge is incalculable. It is bordered, not by a hedge, but by uneven and in places
bushy wastes, often as wide as a field. The
wastes, of course, are divided from the cultivated
slopes below by hedges, but either these are low,
as on the right, or they are irregularly expanded
into thickets of yew and blackthorn, and even into
beech plantations, as on the left. Whoever cares
to rides or walks here instead of on the dust. A goat
or two were feeding here. There was, and there
nearly always is, an encampment of gypsies. The

telegraph posts and the stout, three-sided, old, white
milestones stand here.   The telegraph posts, in one
place, for some distance alternate with low, thick
yew trees.   I liked those telegraph posts, business-
like and mysterious, and their wires that are sufficient of themselves to create the pathetic fallacy.
None the less, I liked the look of the gypsies camping under them.   If they were not there, in fact,
they would have to be invented.   They are at
home there.   See them at nightfall, with their
caravans drawn up facing the wind, and the men
by the half-door at the back smoking, while the
hobbled horses are grazing and the children playing near.   The children play across the road, motor
cars or no motor cars, laughing at whoever amuses
them.   There were two caravans at the highest
point near Puttenham, where the ridge is so narrow
that the roadside thicket is well below the road,
and I saw clear to Hindhead: in another place
there were two antique, patched tents on hoops.

The wind was now strong in my face again.   But
it did not rain, and at moments the sun had the
power to warm.   There was not a moment when
I had not a lark singing overhead.   On the right
hand slope, which is more gradual than that to the
left, men were rolling some grass fields, harrowing
others; lower down they were ploughing.   Men

were beginning to work among the hop poles on
the left. The oaks in the woods there were each
individualized, and had a smoky look which they
would not have had in Summer, Autumn, or Winter.

Houses very seldom intrude on the waste, and
there are few near it. On the south side two or
three big houses had been built so as to command
Hindhead, etc., and a board directed me to the
" Jolly Farmer " at Puttenham, but no inn was
visible till I came to the " Victory," which was
well past the half-way mark to Farnham. The
north side showed not more than a cottage or two,
until I began to descend towards Farnham and
came to a villa which had trimmed the waste outside its gates and decorated it with the inscription,
" Keep off the grass." Going downhill was too
much of a pleasure for me to look carefully at Run-
fold, though I noticed another " Jolly Farmer "
there, and a " Princess Royal," with the date
1819. This not very common sign put into my
head the merry song about the " brave *Princess
Royal* " that set sail from Gravesend—

" On the tenth of December and towards the year's end,"

and met a pirate, who asked them to " drop your
main topsail and heave your ship to," but got
the answer,—

" We'll drop our main topsail and heave our ship to,
  But that in some harbour, not alongside of you.
  So we hoisted the royals and set the topsail,
  And the brave *Princess Royal* soon showed them her tail :
    And we went a-cruising, and we went a-cruising,
    And we went a-cruising, all on the salt seas."

The good tune and merry words lasted me down
among the market gardens and florists' plantations,
past the " Shepherd and Flock " at the turning to
Moor Park, to the Wey again, and the first oast-
house beside it, and so into Farnham at a quarter
to nine, which I felt to be breakfast time.

While I drank my coffee the rising wind slammed
a door and the first shower passed over. The sun
shone for me to go to the " Jolly Farmer " across
the Wey, in a waterside street of cottages and
many inns, such as the " Hop Bag," the " Bird
in Hand," and the " Lamb."   The " Jolly Farmer,"
Cobbett's birthplace, a small inn standing back a
little, with a flat black and white front, was labelled
" Cobbett's Birthplace," in letters as big as are
usually given to the name of a brewer.   It is built
close up against a low sandy bank, which continues
above the right shore of the Wey, somewhat conspicuously, for miles.   Behind the " Jolly Farmer "
this bank is a cliff, hollowed out into caves (no one
knows how old, or whether made by Druids or
smugglers), and overgrown by bushes and crowned

6

by elms full of rooks' nests. The whole of this
waterside is attractive, rustic, but busy. The
Wey is already a strong stream there, and timber
yards and warehouses abut on it. A small public
garden occupies the angle made by one of its
willowy bends.

Farnham West Street was for the moment warm
in the sun as I walked slowly between its shops to
where the porched brick fronts of decent old houses
were scarcely interrupted by a quiet shop or two
and the last inns, the " Rose and Thistle " and the
" Holly Bush." It is one of those streets in which
a hundred houses have been welded into practically
one block. There are some very old houses, some
that are old, and some not very old, but all together compose one long, uneven wall of rustic
urbanity. Castle Street is entirely different. It
takes its name from the Bishop of Winchester's
castle, a palace of old red brick and several cedars
standing at its upper end. Being about three times
as broad as West Street, it is fit to be compared for
breadth with the streets of Marlborough, Wootton
Bassett, or Epsom. Most of the houses are private
and not big, of red or of plastered or whitened
brick ; but there is a baker's shop, a " Nelson's
Arms," and a row of green-porched alms-houses.
At the far end the street rises and curves a little

to the left, and is narrowed by the encroachment
of front gardens only possessed by the houses at
that point.   A long flight of steps above this curve
ascends a green slope of arum and ivy and chestnut trees, past an old episcopal fruit wall, to a
rough-cast gateway, with clock and belfry, and
beyond that, the palace and two black, many-
storied cedars towering at its front door.

I looked in vain for a statue of Cobbett in Farnham.   Long may it be before there is one, for it will
probably be bad and certainly unnecessary.   So
long as " Rural Rides " is read he needs not to
share that kind of resurrection of the just with
Queen Anne and the late Dukes of Devonshire
and of Cambridge.   The district has bred yet another man who combines the true countryman
and the writer.   I mean, of course, George Bourne,
author of "The Bettesworth Book," a volume which
ought to go on to the most select shelf of country books, even beside those of White, Cobbett,
Jefferies, Hudson, and Burroughs.   Bettesworth was
a Surrey labourer, a neighbour and workman of
the author's.   He was an observant and communi-
cative man : his employer took notes from time
to time, and the book is mainly a record of conversations.   George Bourne gives a brief setting to
the old man's words, yet a sufficient one.   Pain

and sorrow are not absent, and afar off we see a
gray glimpse of the workhouse ; but the whole is
joyful.   Even when Bettesworth " felt a bit Christ-
massy " there is no melancholy ; his head merely
seems " all mops and brooms."   His wife tells him
that he has been laughing in his sleep.   " I was
always laughing, then," he says, " until I was sore
all round wi' it."   We have Bettesworth's own
words in most cases, and George Bourne never in-
terferes except to help.   There is no insipid contrast with the outer world, though here and there
we have an echo from it ; we hear of railways as
not particularly convenient, and a dull way of
travelling ; and of cut-purses, " got up they was,
ye know, reg'lar fly-looking blokes, like gentlemen."
Nothing is omitted but what had to be.   Bettesworth cleaned cesspools at times, and the best
things in the book centre round his " excellent
versatility in usefulness."   Well-sinking, reaping,
lawn-mowing, pole-pulling in the hop garden, mending of roofs and steeples, and all the glorious
activities connected with horses, had come into his
work : as for adventure, he drove his first pair of
cart horses from Staines to Smithfield Market.   He
had been a wanderer, too.   During a long absence
from friends he wrote to a brother, enclosing a gift;
but on the way to the post he met an acquaintance,

" and I ast'n if he'd 'ave a drink. So when he says yes, I took the letter an' tore out the dollar an' chucked the letter over the hedge. An' we went off an' 'ad a bottle o' rum wi' this dollar. An' that's all as they ever heerd o' me for seven year."

But the conversations themselves were held while Bettesworth was laying turf, or during the quite genial fatigue following a fifteen-hour day. " Laying Turf " is one of the most charming pieces in the world. The old steeple-mender, reaper, and carter was laying turf under continuous rain and in an uncomfortable attitude, and made the unexpected comment : " Pleasant work this. I could very well spend my time at it, with good turfs."

"The Bettesworth Book " appeared in 1901. "Memoirs of a Surrey Labourer," the record of Bettesworth's last years—1892–1905—appeared in 1907. At first the book may seem tame, a piece of reporting which leaves the reader not unaware of the notebooks consulted by the author. But in the end comes a picture out of the whole, painfully, dubiously emerging, truthful undoubtedly, subtle, not easy to understand, which raises George Bourne to a high place among observers. Apart from his observation, too, he shows himself a man with a ripe and generous, if staid, view of life, and a writer capable of more than accurate writing : witness

his picture of frozen rime on telegraph wires, of
Bettesworth's "polling beck" or potato fork, and
phrases like this: "Near the beans there were
brussels sprouts, their large leaves soaked with
colour out of the clouded day."

Bettesworth had fought in the Crimea, and during
sixty years had been active unceasingly over a
broad space of English country—Surrey, Sussex,
and Hampshire—always out of doors. His memory was good, his eye for men and trades a vivid
one, and his gift of speech unusual, "with swift
realistic touch, convincingly true;" so that a picture of rural England during the latter half of the
nineteenth century, by one born in the earlier half
and really belonging to it, is the result. The por-
trait of an unlettered pagan English peasant is
fascinating. He lived in a parish where people of
urban habits were continually taking the place of
the older sort who dropped out, but he had himself been labourer, soldier, "all sorts of things;
but . . . first and last by taste a peasant, with
ideas and interests proper to another England than
that in which we are living now," and perhaps
unconscious of the change since the days when
he saw four men in a smithy making an axe-head:
"Three with sledge-'ammers, and one with a little
'ammer, tinkin' on the anvil . . . There was one

part of making a axe as they'd never let anybody see 'em at."

The talk, and George Bourne's comments reveal this man's way of thinking and speaking, his lonely thoughts, and his attitude in almost every kind of social intercourse. They show his physical strength, his robust and gross enjoyment, his isolation, his breeding and independence, his tenderness without pity, his courage, his determination to endure. No permissible amount of quotation can explain the subtle appeal of his talk, for example, whilst turf-laying,—

" Half unawares it came home to me, like the contact of the garden mould, and the smell of the earth, and the silent saturation of the cold air. You could hardly call it thought—the quality in this simple prattling. Our hands touching the turfs had no thought either; but they were alive for all that; and of such a nature was the life in Bettesworth's brain, in its simple touch upon the circumstances of his existence. The fretful echoes men call opinions did not sound in it; clamour of the daily press did not disturb its quiet; it was no bubble puffed out by learning, nor indeed had it any of the gracefulness which some mental life takes from poetry and art; but it was still a genuine and strong elemental life of the human

brain that during those days was my companion.
It seemed as if something very real, as if the true
sound of the life of the village had at last reached
my dull senses."

It will now reach duller senses than George
Bourne's. No one has told better how a peasant
who has not toned his other virtues with thrift is
deserted in the end by God and even the majority
of men. The "Memoirs" are shadowed from the
first by the helplessness of Bettesworth's epileptic
wife. The whole of his last year was a dimly lighted,
solitary, manly agony. . . . Now, a statue of Fred-
erick Bettesworth might well be placed at the foot
of Castle Street, to astonish and annoy, if a sculptor
could be found.

As I was passing the "Jolly Sailor" and its jolly
signboard; a gypsy, a sturdy, black-haired, and
brown - faced woman, was coming into Farnham
carrying a basket packed tight with daffodils. The
sun shone and was warm, but the low road was still
wet. It was the Pilgrim's Way now, not merely a
parallel road such as I had been on since Dorking.
For some miles it kept the Wey in sight, and over
beyond the river, that low wall and ledge of sand,
used by the railway, crested with oak and pine here
and there, and often dappled on its slope with gorse.
The land on my right was different, being largely

sodden, bare, arable, with elms.   But it was a pleasure to ride and walk and always to see the winding
river and its willows, and that even green terrace now
near, now far.   Looking across at this scene were
a number of detached houses, old and new, at good
intervals along the right hand side of the road :
some of them could see also the long Alice Holt
woods of oaks and larches, the tips of certain small
groups of trees gilded fitfully by the sunshine.   At
Willey Mill, soon after leaving Farnham, the road
actually touched the river, and horses can walk
through it parallel to the road and cool their feet ;
and just past this, I entered Hampshire.   More
often the river was midway between my road and
the terrace, touching an old farm-house of brick and
timber in the plashy meadows, or turning a mill
with a white plunge of water under sycamores.
But the gayest and most springlike sign was the
fresh whitewash on every fruit tree in an orchard
by the wayside; it suggested a festival.   The poles
were being set up in the hop gardens.   The hedges
enclosing them had been allowed to grow up to a
great height for a screen against wind, and to make
a diaphanous green wall.   Many were the buildings
related to hops, whose mellow brickwork seemed to
have been stained by a hundred harvests.

Bentley, the first village in Hampshire, seemed

hardly more than a denser gathering, and all on the
right hand, of the houses that had been scattered
along since Farnham, with the addition of two inns
and of a green which a brooklet crosses and turns
into a pond at the road's edge. After Bentley the
road ascended, the place of houses was taken by
trees, chiefly lines of beeches connected with several
embowered mansions at some distance, one of pale
stone, one of dark brick. Several rookeries inhabited
these beeches. Froyle House, perhaps the chief in
this neighbourhood, stood near where the road is
highest, and yet closest to the river—a many-gabled
pale house next to a red church tower among elms
and black-flamed cypresses. Up to the church and
house a quarter of a mile of grass mounted, with
some isolated ancient thorns and many oaks, which
in one spot near the road gathered together into a
loose copse. The park itself ran with not too conspicuous or regular a boundary into hop gardens
and ploughland. A low wall on a bank separated
it from the road, and where a footpath had to pass
the wall the stile was a slab of stone pierced by two
pairs of foot-holes, approached up the bank by three
stone steps. It was here, and at eleven, that I
first heard the chiffchaff saying, " Chiff-chaff, chiff-
chaff, chiff-chaff, chiff! " A streamlet darted out
of the park towards the Wey, and on the other side

of the road, and below it, had to itself a little steep coomb of ash trees. An oak had been felled on the coomb side, and a man was clearing the brushwood round it, but the small bird's double note, almost as regular as the ticking of a clock, though often coming to an end on the first half, sounded very clear in the coomb. He sang as he flitted among the swaying ash tops in that warm, cloudy sun. I thought he sang more shrilly than usual, something distractedly. But I was satisfied. Nothing so convinces me, year after year, that Spring has come and cannot be repulsed, though checked it may be, as this least of songs. In the blasting or dripping weather which may ensue, the chiffchaff is probably unheard; but he is not silenced. I heard him on March 19 when I was fifteen, and I believe not a year has passed without my hearing him within a day or two of that date. I always expect him and always hear him. Not all the blackbirds, thrushes, larks, chaffinches, and robins can hide the note. The silence of July and August does not daunt him. I hear him yearly in September, and well into October—the sole Summer voice remaining save in memory. But for the wind I should have heard him yesterday. I went on more cheerfully, as if each note had been the hammering of a tiny nail into Winter's coffin.

My road now had the close company of the railway, which had crossed the river. The three ran side by side on a strip not more than a quarter of a mile in breadth; but the river, small, and not far from its source, was for the most part invisible behind the railway. Close to the railway bank some gypsies had pitched a tent, betrayed by the scarlet frock of one of the children. But in a moment scarlet abounded. The hounds crossing road and railway in front of me were lost to sight for several minutes before they reappeared on the rising fields towards Binsted Wyck. The riders, nearly all in scarlet, kept coming in for ten minutes or so from all hands, down lanes, over sodden arable land, between hop gardens, past folded sheep. Backwards and forwards galloped the scarlet before the right crossing of the railway was taken. The fox died in obscurity two miles away.

How warm and sweet the sun was can be imagined when I say that it made one music of the horn-blowing, the lambs' bleating, the larks' singing, as I sat looking at Bonham's Farm. This plain old brick house, with fourteen windows—two dormers —symmetrically placed, fronted the road down two or three hundred yards of straight, hedged cart track. It had spruce firs on the left, on the right some beeches and a long barn roof stained ochre by lichens.

Then I came to Holybourne. It is a village built in a parallelogram formed by a short section of the main road, two greater lengths of parallel by-roads, and a cross road connecting these two. Froyle was of an equally distinct type, lying entirely on a by-road parallel to the main road, near the church and great house, as Bentley lay entirely on one side of the main road, half a mile from its church. Holybourne Church—Holy Rood—stands at the corner where the short cross road joins one of the side roads; where it joins the other is the Manor Farm. I turned up by the " White Hart " and the smithy and chestnut with which the village begins, and found the church. It is a flint and stone one, with a moderately sharp shingled spire that spreads out at the base. On the side away from the main road, that is northward, lies plough-land mixed with copse rising to the horizon, but, near by, a hop garden, an oast-house, a respectable, square, ivy-mantled farm-house possessing a fruit wall, a farmyard occupied by black pigs, and a long expanse of corrugated iron, roofing old whitestone sheds and outbuildings. Southward is a chalk-bottomed pond of clear water, containing two sallow islets, and bordered, where it touches the road, by

chestnuts, a lime, and an ivy-strangled spruce fir.
This pond is not cut off in any way from the churchyard and all its tombstones of Lillywhites, Warners,
Mays, Fidlers, Knights, Inwoods, and Burninghams.
In the church I saw chiefly two things : the wall
tablet to " George Penton, Brassfounder, Member
of the Worshipful Company of Drapers, who resided in New Street Square, and whose remains
were deposited in St. Bride's parish church,
London," and a slender window decorated
with tiny flowered discs of alternating blue and
orange.

Holybourne's shrubberies, and the beeches and
elms of an overhanging rookery, shadowed and
quieted the main road as if it had been private.
Moreover, there was still some sun to help dapple
the dust with light as well as leaf shadow. Nor
was the wind strong, and what there was
helped me.

Before the village had certainly ended, Alton
had begun. Its grandest building was its first—the
workhouse. It is an oblong brick building lying
back behind its gardens, with a flat ivied front
which is pierced by thirty-three windows, including
dormers, placed symmetrically about a central door,
and an oval stone tablet bearing the figures " 1795."
It smacked of 1795 pure and simple; of the Eng-

land which all the great men of the nineteenth century were born in and nearly all hated. Its ivy, its plain, honest face, and substantial body of mellow red brick, and that date, 1795, gave the workhouse a genial tranquillity which no doubt was illusory. From there to the end of Alton is one not quite straight or quite level street—Normandy Street and High Street—altogether a mile of houses and of shops (including the "Hop Poles," the "Barley Mow," and the "French Horn") that supply everything a man needs, with the further advantage that if a man wants his hair cut he can have it done by Julius Cæsar : the town brews beer, and even makes paper. It is a long and a low town, and the main street has no church in it until it begins to emerge on to the concluding green, called Robin Hood Butts.

I could have gone as well through Medstead as through Ropley to Alresford, but I went by the Ropley way, and first of all through Chawton. Here the road forks at a smithy, among uncrowded thatched cottages and chestnuts and beeches. The village is well aware of the fact that Jane Austen once dwelt in a house at the fork there, opposite the "Grey Friar." I took the right hand road and had a climb of two miles, from 368 feet above sea level to 642 feet. This road ascended, parallel

to the railway, in a straight, narrow groove, and
was fringed on both sides for some distance, up
to and past the highest point, by hedgeless copses
of oak and beech, hazel, thorn, and ivy. An old
chalk pit among the trees had been used for depositing pots and pans, but otherwise the copses
might never have been entered except by the chiff-
chaff that sang there, and seemed to own them.
Once out in the open at Four Marks, I had spread
out around me a high but not hilly desolation of
gray grass, corrugated iron bungalows, and chicken-
runs. I glided as fast as possible away from this
towards the Winchester Downs beyond, not pausing even at the tenth milestone from Winchester
to enjoy again that brief broadening on either hand
of the rough wayside turf, sufficient to make a fair
ground. Past the " Chequers " at Ropley Dean,
and again past the " Anchor " towards Bishop's
Sutton, there are similar and longer broadenings ;
and on one of these two tramps were lying asleep,
the one hid by hat and clothes, the other with clear
outstanding pale profile, hands clasped over the
fifth rib, and feet stuck up, like a carved effigy.
I was as glad to see them sleeping in the sun as to
hear the larks singing. I would have done the
same if I had been somebody else.

Bishop's Sutton, the next village, resembles Holy-

bourne in the shrubberies with which it hushes the
road. Passing the "Plough" and the "Ship"
(kept by a man with the great Hampshire name of
Port), I went into the church, which was decorated
by the memorial tablets of people named Wright
and an eighteenth century physician named William
Cowper, and by daffodils and primroses arranged in
moss and jam jars. Many dead flowers were littered about the floor. The churchyard was better,
for it had a tree taller than the tower, and another
lying prone alongside the road for children to play
on, and very few tombstones. Of these few, one
recorded the deaths of three children in 1827–1831,
and furthermore thus boldly baffled the infidel,—

"Bold infidelity, turn pale and die.
Beneath this sod three infants' ashes lie.
Say, are they lost or sav'd?
If Death's by sin, they sinn'd, for they lie here:
If Heaven's by works, in Heaven they can't appear.
Ah, reason, how depraved!
Revere the Bible's sacred page, for there the knot's untied."

The children were Oakshotts, a Hampshire name
borne by a brook and a hanger near Hawkley.

The telegraph wires were whining as if for rain
as I neared Alresford, having on my right hand the
willowy course of the young Alre, and before me
its sedgy, wide waters, Old Alresford pond. The
road became Alresford by being lined for a third

7

of a mile downhill by cottages, inns, and shops.
This is the whole town, except for one short, very
broad turning half way along at the highest point,
and opposite where the church stands bathed in
cottages.

Alresford is an excellent little town, sad-coloured
but not cold, and very airy.   For not only does the
main street descend from this point steeply west
towards Winchester, but the broad street also
descends northward, so that over the tops of the
houses crossing the bottom of it and over the
hidden Alre, are seen the airy highlands of Abbots-
stone, Swarraton, and Godsfield.   The towered flint
church and the churchyard make almost as much
of a town as Alresford itself, so numerous are the
tombs of all the Wools, Keanes, Corderoys, Priv-
etts, Cameses, Whitears, Norgetts, Dykeses, scattered among many small yew trees.   At one side
stand many headstones of French officers who had
served Napoleon, but died in England about the
time of Waterloo—Lhuille, Lavan, Garnier, Riouffe,
and Fournier.   Inside the church one of the most
noticeable things is a tablet to one John Lake, who
was born in 1691, died in 1759, and lies near that
spot, waiting for the day of judgment.   " *Qualis
erat*," says the inscription, "*dies iste indicabit :* "
(" What manner of man he was that day will make

known.") The writer of these words saved himself from lies and from trouble.

I looked in vain for any one bearing the name of the poet who praised Alresford pond—George Wither. Or, rather, he praised it as it was in the days when Thetis resorted thither and played there with her attendant fishes, and received crowns of flowers and beech leaves from the land nymphs at eve :—

" For pleasant was that pool, and near it then
Was neither rotten marsh nor boggy fen.
It was not overgrown with boist'rous sedge,
Nor grew there rudely then along the edge
A bending willow nor a prickly bush,
Nor broad-leaf'd flag, nor reed, nor knotty rush ;
But here, well order'd, was a grove with bowers :
There grassy plots set round about with flowers.
Here you might through the water see the land
Appear, strow'd o'er with white or yellow sand.
Yon, deeper was it ; and the wind by whiffs
Would make it rise and wash the little cliffs,
On which oft pluming sat, unfrightened than,
The gaggling wildgoose and the snow-white swan :
With all those flocks of fowls that to this day
Upon those quiet waters breed and play.
For though those excellences wanting be
Which once it had, it is the same that we
By transposition name the Ford of Arle ;
And out of which along a chalky marl
That river trills, whose waters wash the fort
In which brave Arthur kept his royal court."

—Which, being interpreted, means Camelot, or Winchester.

Yet Wither is one of the poets whom we can connect with a district of England and often cannot sunder from it without harm. Many other poets are known to have resided for a long or a short time in certain places; but of these a great many did not obviously owe much to their surroundings, and some of those that did, like Wordsworth, possessed a creative power which made it unnecessary that the reader should see the places, whatever the railway companies may say. Wordsworth at his best is rarely a local poet, and his earth is an "insubstantial fairy place." But if you know the pond at Alresford before this poem, you add a secondary but very real charm to Wither; while, if you read the poem first, you are charmed, if at all, partly because you see that the pond exists, and you taste something of the human experience and affection which must precede the mention. To have met the poet's name here would have been to furbish the charm a little.

The name of Norgett on a stone called up Oldhurst into my mind, a thatched house built of flints in the middle of oak woods not far off—ancient woods where the leaves of many Autumns whirled and rustled even in June. It was three miles from the hard road, and it used to seem that I had travelled

three centuries when at last I emerged from the
oaks and came in sight of that little humped gray
house and within sound of the pines that shadowed
it.   It had a face like an owl; it was looking at
me.   Norgett must have heard me coming from
somewhere among the trees, for, as I stepped into
the clearing at one side, he was at the other.   I
thought of Herne the Hunter on catching sight of
him.   He was a long, lean, gray man with a beard
like dead gorse, buried gray eyes, and a step that
listened.   He hardly talked at all, and only after
questions that he could answer quite simply.   Speech
was an interruption of his thoughts, and never
sprang from them ; as soon as he ceased talking
they were resumed with much low murmuring and
whistling—like that of the pine trees—to himself,
which seemed the sound of their probings in the
vast of himself and Nature.   His was a positive,
an active silence.   It did me good to be with him,
especially after I had learned to share it with
him, instead of trying to get him to join in gossip.
I say I shared it, but what I did and enjoyed was,
apparently, to sleep as we walked.   It was unpleasant to wake up, to go away from that cold,
calm presence.   Then, perhaps, I sneaked back for
a talk with Mrs. Norgett, who was a little, busy
woman with black needle eyes and a needle voice

like a wren's, as thin and lively as a cricket; she knew everything that happened, and much that did not. But with him she also was silent.

These two had two daughters—and, in fact, I got to know them by staying with a friend three miles away, where one of the girls was a servant: she said that there were always woodcocks round Old-hurst, and her father would introduce me. It was several years since I had seen Norgett and Old-hurst, but a letter concerning these daughters brought them again before me,—

" Martha Norgett is dead. I suppose you remember her just as a stout, nervous girl, with uncomfortable manners, tow hair, face always as red as if she had been making toast, gray eyes rather scared but alarmingly frank, always rushing about the house noisily and apologetically at the same time; willing to do anything at any time for almost anybody, but especially for you, perhaps, when you stayed with us in Summer holidays. I am sure you could not tell me offhand how old she was. I can hear you saying, ' Well, the country girls always look much older than you said they were. I suppose it is the responsibility, and they belong to an older, more primitive type. So I always have an instinct to treat them deferentially. . . . She might be twenty-three or -four—

say, eighteen.   But then she was just the same
fifteen years ago. . . . Thirty—thirty-five. That is
absurd. I give it up.' . . .

" I will not tell you her age, but I want to give
you something of Martha's history, though it is
now too late for the development of that instinct
for treating her deferentially.

" The family has been in the parish since the
beginning of the parish register, in 1597. I should
say that 597 would be much nearer the date when
they settled in that clearing among the oaks.
Fifteen centuries is not much to a temperament
like theirs, perhaps.   But they will hardly see
another fifteen : they have not adapted themselves.
Martha and her sister Mary were old Norgett's only
children. I don't think you ever saw Mary. You
would have treated her deferentially. As bright
and sweet as a chaffinch was Mary. She had
small, warm brown eyes that seemed to be dis-
solving in a glow of amused pleasure at everything.
Everybody and everything as a rule conspired to
preserve the glow ; but now and then—cruelly and
very easily—drawing tears from them because then
they were softer than ever, and one could not help
smiling as one wiped the tears away, as if she had
only cried for craft and prettiness.   That was
when she was seven or eight. For a year or so she

was always either laughing or crying. Visitors used to take delight in converting one into the other. They treated her like a bird. She had very thick and long, fine and dark brown hair—such beautiful and lustrous hair! I remember treating it as if it were alive, apart from her life, as if it were a wild creature living on her shoulders.

" She was considered rather a stupid child. Some people seem to regard animals as rather stupid human beings never blessed with spectacles and baldness—it was they who called her stupid. She never said anything wise. Usually she laughed when she spoke, and you could hardly make out the words : to try to read a meaning of an accustomed sort into her speech was little better than making a translation from a brook's song or a bird's song; for in her case also it really meant translating from an unknown tongue. Everybody gave her presents. She had as many dolls as the cat had kittens. She was fond of people, but she seemed fonder of these, and, seeing her, I used to smile and think of the words : ' Ye shall serve gods the work of men's hands, wood and stone, which neither see, nor hear, nor eat, nor smell.'

" There were a hundred differences between her and Martha. Martha had but one doll. It was an old stiff wooden doll, cut by the keeper for his

first-born, and never clothed. Martha kept it in
the wood-lodge, and would not have it in the house,
but went to look at it just once at morning and
once at night, and never missed doing so. She
did not play with Mary's, though as maid-of-all-
work, bustling about seriously and untidily, often
breaking and upsetting things, she treated them
with immense reverence, putting them safely away
in a sitting posture when their mistress was tired
of them and left them on chairs, in the hearth, or
on the table—anywhere. Nobody supposed that
Martha cared anything for her solitary wooden
idol, and if you inquired after it she only looked
awkwardly into your face with those pale eyes and
said nothing, or perhaps asked you if you would
like to see Mary's newest one. She was always busy,
they could not keep her from work; she was
strong, and never ailed or complained. If a baby
was brought to the house, to see Mary's delicate
ways with it was worth a journey; surrounding it
with dolls, and giving herself up to it and taking
good care of it, while Martha slipped away and was
not to be seen. Mary was tenderest hearted, and
could never pass carelessly by anything like a calf's
head thrust out of a hole in a dark shed into the sun.
As for Martha she was too busy, though of course she
would run to the town, if need were, to fetch a vet.

"Mary was not nearly so strong, but she continued to grow in grace and charm. At seventeen I think she was the loveliest human being of her sex that I ever saw. I say of her sex, because she was so absolutely and purely a woman that she seemed a species apart, even to me a mystery; every position of her, every attitude, action, everything she did and did not do, proclaimed her a woman newly created out of the elements which but yesterday made her a child, an animal or bird in human form. Many would have liked to marry her. Her round soft chin, her rather long, and not too thin, smiling mouth, her living hair, her wild eyes, won her lovers wherever she was seen. And yet I had a feeling that she would not marry. . . . However, I came back from Italy one year to find her married to a young farmer near Alton.

"Martha had already been with us for some years. When Mary began to have babies Martha was over at the farm as often as possible. Mary grew paler and thinner, but not less beautiful, and hardly less gay and childlike. She did as she pleased—always perfectly dressed, while others, and, above all, Martha, busied themselves in a hundred ways for her and her baby. Now that she was obviously delicate as well as beautiful, her hair looked more than ever like a wild life of some kind affectionately attached to her. Martha worked harder for her, if that were possible, than for us. I have heard her panting away as she swept the stairs and sometimes sighing, too, but never stopping for that luxury, and her sister would call out and laughingly chide her for it, to which she replied with another laugh, not ceasing to pant or to sweep. Mary was adored by her husband.

" Few men, I should say, took notice of Martha. She was very abrupt with them, and had nothing to say if they spoke out of a wish to be agreeable. Now and then she reported some advance— a soldier, for example, offered to carry her parcels home for her at night; but as soon as they turned from the high road into our dark lane she found an excuse, swept up all the parcels into her arms and was off without a word. Another time she allowed herself to be taken home on several evenings by a young man whose real sweetheart was away for a time : he had told her the fact, and politely asked if she would like him to take her home in the interval. What Martha wanted was a baby. She was the laughing-stock of the kitchen for confessing it. She did not mind : she stitched away at baby's underclothing which all went for her sister's infants, but was meant for her own. She once bought a cradle at an auction sale—do you

feel deferential now ?   Yet one man she put off
by telling him she already had a lover.

" Did you ever hear of her one dream ?   She came
in and told us in great excitement that she had had
a dream. She said, ' It was as plain as plain, and
all the family were eating boiled potatoes with
their fingers except me. Law, mum, that ever I
should have dreamed such a thing.' . . . She blushed
that the family should have been put to shame in
a dream of hers.

" At last we heard that she had a lover. Her
fellow servants accused her of doing the courting,
and he was younger than she. She was not impatient, even now. When she heard that we were
to move in a year's time, she made up her mind
that she must go to the new house and see what
it was like living there. ' He's not so bad,' she said
quietly. ' Father and mother think the world of
him. It's not love. Oh, no ! I'm too old for that,
and I won't have any nonsense. But he says he'll
marry me. We shall love after that, maybe ; but
if not, there'll be the children. We shall have a nice
little home. Charley has bought a mirror, and he
is saving up for a ring with a real stone in it.' And
so she went on soberly, yet perhaps madly.

" We moved, and Martha with us. She had to
wait still longer, because Mary was expecting

another child. Mary was not so well as usual. She was very thin, and yet looked in a way younger than ever. Martha left us to devote herself to her sister. I went over once or twice : I wish now it had been oftener. Martha looked the same as ever. Mary grew still more frail, until, in a ghastly way, you could not see her body for her soul, as the poet says. Her husband being called away left her confidently in Martha's hands.

" The nearest doctor was five miles off. She had to go for him suddenly in a night of winter thunder. The whole night was up in arms, the black clouds and the woods, the noises of a great wind and thunder trying to get the better of one another, and the rain drowning the lightning as if it had been no more than an eel in a dirty pond, and drowning thunder and the wind at last. When Martha reached the doctor's house he was out. She found another, and having meekly delivered her message was gone before the man could offer to drive her back with him ; but the horse was so helpless in the stormy, steep, crooked roads among the woods that he expected to find her there before him. When he arrived Mary was delirious, speaking of her sister, whom she seemed to see approaching and at last coming into the room ; she cried out, ' Martha ! ' and never spoke again. Martha had not returned.

The cowman found her lying on her face in the
mire by a gateway, stopped in her swift, clumsy
running by heart-failure, dead. Poor old Martha!
but I have no doubt she was quite happy making
for that green blind upstairs in her sister's house,
hastening half asleep, and only waking up as she
stumbled over the stile. The world misses her—
and her children."

I had never met the surname before, and here
upon a stranger's tombstone it called up Martha
like a mysterious incantation.

The tune of the telegraph wires became sadder,
and I pushed on with the purpose of getting as
far as possible before the rain fell. The road out
of Alresford is dignified by a long avenue of elms,
with a walk between, lining it on the right as far
as the gate of Arlebury House. Opposite the last
of the trees it was a pleasure to see on a wayside
plot, where elms mingled with telegraph posts, a
board advertising building sites, but leaning awry,
mouldy, and almost illegible. Then the road went
under the railway and bent south-westwards, while
I turned to the right to follow a byway along the
right bank of the Itchen, where there was a village
every two or three miles, and I could be sure of
shelter. The valley, a flat-bottomed marshy one,
was full of drab-tufted grasses and new-leafed

willows, and pierced by straight, shining drains.
The opposite bank rose up rather steeply, and was
sometimes covered with copse, sometimes carved
by a chalk pit; tall trees with many mistletoe
boughs grew on top. I got to Itchen Abbas, its
bridge, mill, church, and " Plough," all in a group,
when the rain was beginning. I had not gone much
further when it became clear that the rain was to
be heavy and lasting, and I took shelter in a cart-
lodge. There I was joined by a thatcher and a deaf
and dumb labourer. The thatcher would talk of
nothing but the other man, having begun by ex-
plaining that he could not be expected to say " Good-
afternoon." The deaf man sat on the straw and
watched us. He was the son of a well-to-do farmer,
but had left home because he did not get enough
money and was in other ways imposed on. He had
now been at the same farm thirty years. He was
a good workman, understanding by signs what he
had to do. Moreover, he could read the lips,
though how he learnt—for he could neither read
nor write—I do not know! Probably, said the
thatcher, he knows what we are saying now. At
half-past three the horses came in for the day.
They had begun at half-past six; so, said the
thatcher, " they don't do a man's work." So we
talked while the horses were stabled, and rain fell

and it thundered, if not to the tune of " Green-sleeves," at least to that of blackbirds' songs.

The sky was full and sagging, but actually rained little, when I started soon after four, and went on through the four Worthys,—on my left the low sweep of Easton Down, and the almost window-less high church wall among elms between it and the river ; and on my right, arable country and pewits tumbling over it. Worthy Park, a place of lawns and of elms and chestnuts, adorned the road with an avenue of very branchy elms. At King's Worthy, just beyond, I might have crossed over and taken the shortest way to Salisbury, that is to say, by Stockbridge. But, except at Stockbridge itself, there is hardly a house on the twenty miles of road, and either one inn or two. Evidently the sky could not long contain itself, and as I knew enough of English inns to prefer not arriving at one wet through, I determined to take the Roman road through Headbourne Worthy to Winchester. This brought me through a region of biggish houses, shrubberies, rookeries, motor cars, and carriages, but also down to a brook and a withy bed, and Headbourne Worthy's little church and blunt shingled spire beside it. The blackbirds were singing their best in the hawthorns as I was passing, and in the puddles they were bathing before singing.

Winchester Cathedral appeared and disappeared several times, and above, it slightly to the left, St. Catherine's smooth hill and beechen crown. In one of these views I saw what I had never before noticed, that the top of the cathedral tower is apparently higher than the top of St. Catherine's Hill.

Through the crowd of Winchester High Street I walked, and straight out by the West Gate and the barracks uphill. I meant to use the Romsey road as far as Ampfield, and thence try to reach Dunbridge. The sky was full of rain, though none was falling. It was a mile before I could mount, and then, for some way, the road was accompanied on the right by yew trees. Between these trees I could see the low, half-wooded Downs crossed by the Roman road to Sarum and by hardly any other road. The most insistent thing there was the Farley Tower, perched on a barrow at one of the highest points, to commemorate not the unknown dead but a horse called Beware Chalkpit, who won a race in 1734 after having leaped into a chalkpit in 1733. The eastern scene was lovelier: the clear green Downs above Twyford, Morestead, and Owslebury, four or five miles away; and then the half wooded green wall of Nan Trodd's Hill which the road curves under to Hursley. But, first, I

8

had to dip down to Pitt Village, which is a small cluster of thatched cottages, mud walls, and beech trees, with a pond and a bright white chalk pit, all at the bottom of a deep hollow. I climbed out of it and glided down under Nan Trodd's Hill and its black yews, divided from the road only by a gentle rise of arable; and so, betwixt a similar but slighter yew-crowned rise and the oaks of Hursley Park, I approached Hursley. The first thing was a disused pump on the right, with an ivy-covered shelter and a fixed lamp; but before the first house there was a beech copse, and after that a farm and its attendant ricks and cottages, and at length the village. A single row of houses faced the park and its rookery beeches through a parallel row of pollard limes; but the centre was a double row of neat brick and timber houses, both old and new, a smithy, a doctor's, and a " King's Head " and " Dolphin." Here also stood the spired church, opposite a branching of roads. At the beginning, middle, and end of the village, gates led into Hursley Park. And I think it was here that I saw the last oast-house in Hampshire.

Immediately after passing the fifth milestone from Winchester I turned with the Romsey road south-west instead of keeping on southward to Otterbourne. It was now darkening and still. I was on a low moist road overhung by oak trees, through which I saw, on the right, a mile away, the big many-windowed Hursley House among its trees. The road had obviously once had wide grassy margins. The line of the old hedge was marked, several yards within a field on the right, by the oaks, the primroses, and the moss, growing there and not beyond: in a wood that succeeded, it was equally clear. The primroses glimmered in the dank shadow of the trees, where the old hedge had been, and round the water standing in old wayside pits. In one place on the left, by Ratlake, the fern and gorse looked like common. Nobody was using the road except the blackbirds and robins. Hardly a house was to be seen. It might have been the edge of the New Forest. If the road could have gone on so, with no more rise and fall, for ever, I think I should have been content. The new church and its pine, and cypress, and laurel, intruded but did not break the charm. More to my taste was the pond on the other side; gorse came to its edge, oaks stood about it, and dabchicks were diving in its unrippled surface. The " White Hart " farther on tempted me. It lay rather below the road on the left, behind the yellow courtyard and the signboard, forming a quadrangle with the stables and sheds on either side. The pale walls and the broad bay window on the ground floor offered "Accommodation for Cyclists." But I did not stop, perhaps because Ampfield House on the other side took away my thoughts from inns. This was an ivy-mantled brick house, like two houses side by side, not very far back from the road; its high blossoming fruit wall bounded the road. Travelling so easily, I was loth to dismount, and on the signpost on the right, near the third milestone from Romsey, I read MSBURY without thinking of Timsbury, which lay on my way to Dunbridge. I glided on for half a mile before thinking better of it, and turning back, discovered my mistake. Here I entered a gravelly, soft road among trees. I should have done well to put up in one of the woodmen's shelters here under the oaks. These huts were frames of stout green branches thatched with hazel peelings and walled with fagots. One was built so that an oak divided its entrance in two, and against the tree was fastened a plain wooden contrivance for gripping and bending wood. Inside, it had other hurdlemaker's implements—a high wooden horse for gripping and bending, and a low wooden table. White peelings were thickly strewn around the huts. The floor showed likewise such signs of life as cigarette ends, matchboxes, and a lobster's claw. On Saturday evening a marsh-tit and a robin alone seemed to have anything to do with them. Nevertheless I went contentedly on between mossy banks, hedges of beech, rhododendrons, and woodlands of oak, beech, and larch, which opened out in one place to show me the fern and pine of Ganger Common. The earth was quiet, dark, and beautiful. The owl was beginning to hunt over the fields, while the blackbird finished his song. Pleasant were the yellow road, the roadside bramble and brier hoops, the gravel pits and gorse at corners. But the sky was wild, threatening the earth both with dark clouds impending and with momentary wan gleams between them, angrier than the clouds. Some rain sprinkled as I dipped down between roadside oaks and a narrow orchard to Brook Farm. Here the road forded a brook, and a lane turned off, with a gravelly bluff on one side, farmyard and ricks on the other. Up in the pale spaces overhead Venus glared like a madman's eye. Yet the rain came to nothing, and for a little longer the few scattered house lights appearing and disappearing in the surrounding country were mysteriously attractive. And then arrived complete darkness and rain together, as I reached the turning where I could see the chimney stack of Michelmersh. I tried the " Malt House " on the left. They could not give me a bed because

" the missus was expecting some friends." I
pushed on against wind and rain to the " Bear and
Ragged Staff," a bigger inn behind a triangle of
rushy turf and a walnut tree. " Accommodation for
Cyclists " was announced, which I always used to
assume meant that there was a bed ; but it does
not. It was raining, hailing, and blowing furiously,
but they could not give me a bed because they were
six in family : no, not any sort of a bed. They
directed me to the " Mill Arms " at Dunbridge.
Crossing the Test by Kim Bridge Mill, the half-
drowned fields smelt like the sea. The mill-house
windows shone above the double water plunging
away into blackness. Then, for a space, when I
had turned sharply north-westward the wind helped
me. Actually I was now at the third inn. They
were polite and even smiling, but they informed me
that I could by no means have a bed, seeing that
the lady and gentleman from somewhere had all
the beds. Nor could they tell me of a bed anywhere,
because it was Easter and people with a spare room
mostly had friends. Luckily a train was just
starting which would bear me away from Dunbridge
to Salisbury. I boarded it, and by eight o'clock I
was among the people who were buying and selling
fish and oranges to the accompaniment of much
chaffing, but no bad temper, in Fish Row. And,

soon, though not at once, I found a bed and a place
to sit and eat in, and to listen to the rain breaking
over gutters and splashing on to stones, and pipes
swallowing rain to the best of their ability, and
signboards creaking in the wind; and to reflect
on the imperfection of inns and life, and on the
spirit's readiness to grasp at all kinds of unearthly
perfection such, for instance, as that which had
encompassed me this evening before the rain. At
that point a man entered whom I slowly recognized
as the liberator of the chaffinch on Good Friday.
At first I did not grasp the connection between this
dripping, indubitably real man and the wraith of
the day before. But he was absurdly pleased to
recognize me, bowing with a sort of uncomfortable
graciousness and a trace of a cockney accent. His
expression changed in those few moments from
a melancholy and too yielding smile to a pale,
thin-lipped rigidity. I did not know whether to
be pleased or not with the reincarnation, when he
departed to change his clothes.

This Other Man, as I shall call him, ate his
supper in silence, and then adjusted himself in the
armchair, stretching himself out so that all of him
was horizontal except his head. He was smoking
a cigarette dejectedly, for he had left his pipe
behind at Romsey. I offered him a clay pipe. No ;

he would not have it. They stuck to his lips, he said. But he volunteered to talk about clay pipes, and the declining industry of manufacturing them. He seemed to know all about ten-inch and fifteen-inch pipes, from the arrival of the clay out of Cornwall in French gray blocks to the wetting of the clay and the beating of it up with iron rods; the rough first moulding of the pipes by hand, and the piercing of the stems; the baking in moulds, the scraping of rough edges by girls, down to the sale of the pipes in the two months round about Christmas to Aldershot, Portsmouth, and such places. These longer pipes, at any rate, have become chiefly ceremonious and convivial, though personally I have hardly ever seen them smoked except by literary people under thirty. No wonder that in one of the principal factories only one artist is left, as the Other Man declared, to pierce the stems with unerring thrust. It seemed to him wonderful that even one man could be found to push a wire up the core of a long thin stick of clay. He had never himself been able to avoid running the wire out at the side before reaching the end. The great man who always succeeded had once made him a pipe with five bowls.

He could not tell me why the industry is decaying. But two causes seem at least to have contributed.

First, a great many of the men who used to smoke
clays smoke cheap cigarettes.   Second, those who
have not taken to cigarettes smoke briar pipes.
Cigarettes appear to give less trouble than pipes.
Any one, drunk or sober, can light them and keep
them alight. They can be put out at any moment
and returned to the cigarette case or tucked behind
the ear. Also, it is held by snobs as well as by haters
of foul pipes that cigarettes are more genteel, or
whatever the name is of our equivalent vice.   But
if a pipe is to be smoked, the briar is believed to
cast some sort of faint credit on the smoker which
the clay does not. That Tennyson used clays probably now only influences a small number of young
men—and that but for a year or two—of a class
that would not take to clays as a matter of course.
A few others of the same class begin in imitation
of labourer, sailor, or gamekeeper, with whom they
have come in exhilarating contact ; and, in turn,
others imitate them. The habit so gained, however,
is not likely to endure. Nearly every one sheds
it, either because he really does not enjoy it, or
he has for some reason to keep it in abeyance too
long for it to be resumed, or he supposes himself
to be conspicuous and prefers not to be.

In the first place he may have been moved partly
by a desire to be conspicuous, to signalize his

individuality by a visible symbol, but such can seldom be a conscious motive with the most self-conscious of men. For some years I met plenty of youths of my own age who were experimenting with clay pipes, nervously colouring small thorny ones, or lying back and making of themselves cushions for long churchwardens, or carrying the bowl of a two-inch pipe upside down like a navvy. But I was never much tempted myself until I went to live permanently in the country. As I was pretty frequently walking at lunch time I took that meal at an inn, and one day remembering that as a child I had got clays from a publican for nothing I asked for one with my beer, and got it. I shall not pretend that this pipe was in any way remarkable, for I have no recollection of it. All I know is that it was not the last. Most, if not all, of my briar pipes at the time were foul. I took more and more to smoking clay pipes when I was alone or where it would not attract attention.

It was not long before I made the discovery that there are clays and clays. Those given away or sold for a halfpenny by innkeepers between the North and South Downs were usually thin and straight, sometimes embellished with a design in relief, particularly with a horned head and the initial letters of the Royal Antediluvian Order of

Buffaloes. Many and many a one of these mere smoking utensils was broken very soon in my teeth or in my pocket, or discarded because I did not like the feel or look of it, or simply because it was an unnecessary addition to my supply. For a time I could and did smoke almost anything, fortified possibly by a feeling (though I cannot recall it) that the custom was worth persisting in. At any rate it was persisted in.

If I pursued singularity I was not blindfold. Not many weeks were occupied in learning that thin clays were useless, or were not for me. They began by burning my tongue, and they were very soon bitten through. On the other hand, thickness alone was not sufficient. For example, Irish pipes up to a third of an inch thick were as rapidly bitten through as the harder thin clays. It was necessary to fit them with mouth-pieces connected by a tin band, and since these would corrode, I refused them. Even a clay that was hard as well as thick was not therefore faultless. I kept one for several years, at intervals trying to make terms with it on account of its good shape—the bowl set at more than a right angle to the stem, and adorned with a conventional ribbed leaf underneath—but always in vain; the clay, being hard after the manner of flint, gritted on the teeth and was no sweeter at the tenth than at the first pipe.

Wherever I went I bought a clay pipe or two. The majority were indifferent. Only after a time was the goodness of the good ones manifest, and by then I might be a hundred miles away from the shop, if I had not forgotten where it came from. These I did everything to preserve. Some of them went through the purification of fire a score of times before they came to an end by falling or, which was rare, by being worn too short. They had the great virtue of being hard, without being stony. They resembled bone in their close grain, sometimes being as smooth as if glazed. But I had little to do with the glazed " colouring " clays. They stank, and I was not ambitious except of achieving a cool, everlasting, and perfectly shaped pipe.

How to use the fire on a foul pipe was learnt by very slow degrees. Many a good pipe cracked or flaked in the flames. They had, I was at last to discover, been too suddenly submitted to great heat. If it was done gradually, the fiercest heat could be and should be imposed on them : they lay pinkish white in the heart of the fire until they possessed more than their original purity. A few of the best would emerge with almost an old ivory hue all over. Some I remember breaking when they had come

safely out and were nearly cool, by tapping them
to shake out the fur. Most of them were toughened
as well as sweetened in the process.

How very rare were those good pipes ! Probably
I did not find more than one in twelve months,
though I bought scores. I was continually trying
Irish clays in a stupid hope that they would not
be bitten through. The best pipe in the majority
of shops was merely one that was not bad. It did
not burn *much ;* it was not bitten through until
it was just reaching its ripeness.

Perhaps I should have remembered more varieties
of goodness and badness had I not twelve months
ago met a perfect clay pipe. It is so hard that I
have only once bitten one through, yet it is soft to
the teeth and tongue. Nor is it very thick ; the
bowl in particular I should have been inclined at
first sight to condemn as too thin. It is smooth,
in fact polished. Its shape is graceful ; the stem
slightly curved, slightly flattened, but thickening
and developing roundness where it *becomes* rather
than joins the bowl, into which it flows so as to form
something like a calabash. There are other shapes
of this excellent material.

This perfect clay pipe came from a shop at
Oxford. A month later I bought some of the
same kind, but an inferior shape, at Melksham.

Everywhere else I have looked in vain for them. I have never seen any one else smoking them who had not got them from me.

Tastes differ, but in this matter I cannot believe that any one capable of distinguishing one clay from another would deny this one's excellence.

The Other Man cared nothing for the matter. He awoke from the stupor to which he had been reduced by listening, and asked,—

" Did you see that weather-vane at Albury in the shape of a pheasant ? or the fox-shaped one by the ford at Butts Green ? or the pub with the red shield and the three tuns and three pairs of wheatsheaves for a sign ? "

" No," I answered, adding what I could remember about the horse's head over the corn chandler's at Epsom. The Other Man had seen this, and also a similar one of white wood over a saddler's at Dorking. He reminded me also of what I was engaged in forgetting—that Shalford had an inn called the " Sea-Horse," and a signboard of a sea-horse with a white head and a fish-like body covered in azure scales. He said it was a better sea-horse than those over the Admiralty gates in Whitehall. Continuing, he asked me why it was that the chief inn of a town was so frequently the " Swan." It was at Leatherhead. It was at

Charing in Kent—I knew that. It was at a score
of other places which I have forgotten. Nor could
I remember a sufficient number of " Lions,"
" Eagles," and " Dolphins " to oppose him. Had
I, was his next question, seen the " Ship " at
Bishop's Sutton, which had a signboard with a
steamer on one side and a sailing ship on the other ?
And not long after this I was asleep.

IV.

BEFORE the first brightening of the light on Sunday morning the rain ceased, and I returned to Dunbridge to pick up the road I had lost on Saturday evening. Above all, I wanted to ride along under Dean Hill, the level-ridged chalk hill dotted with yew that is seen running parallel to the railway a quarter of a mile on your left as you near Salisbury from Eastleigh. The sky was pale, scarcely more blue than the clouds with which it was here and there lightly whitewashed. For five miles I was riding against the stream of the river which rises near Clarendon and meets the Test near Dunbridge. The water and its alders, many of them prostrate, and its drab sedges mingled with intense green and with marsh-marigolds' yellow, were seldom more than a hundred yards away on my right. Pewits wheeled over it with creaking wings and protests against the existence of man.

I did not stop for the villages. Butts Green, for example, where the Other Man had seen the fox weather-vane, began with an old thatched cottage and a big hollow yew, but the green itself was dull, flat, and bare, and the cottages round it newish. Lockerley Green, a mile farther on, was much like it, except that the road traversed instead of skirting the green. Between these two, and beyond Lockerley Church, where the road touched the river and had a fork leading across to East Tytherley, there was a small, but not old, mill, and a miller too, and flour. As I looked back the small sharp spire of the church stuck up over the level ridgy ploughland in a manner which, I supposed, would have made for a religious person a very religious picture. No other building was visible. The railway on my left was more silent than the river on my right, among its willow and alder and tall, tufted grass, at the foot of gorse slopes.

After crossing the railway half a mile past Lockerley Green the road went close to the base of Dean Hill, separated from it by ploughland without a hedge. On the left, that is on the Dean Hill side, stood East Dean Church, a little rustic building of patched brick and plaster walls, mossy roof, and small lead-paned windows displaying the Easter decorations of moss and daffodils. It had a tiny bell turret at the west end, and a round window cut up into radiating panes like a geometrical spider's web. Under the yew tree, amidst long grass,

9

dandelion, and celandine, lay the bones of people bearing the names Edney and Langridge. The door was locked. Its neighbours on the other side of the road were an old cottage with tiled roof and walls of herring-boned brick, smothered from chimney to earth with ivy, in a garden of plum blossom; and next to it, a decent, small home, a smooth clipped block of yew, and a whitewashed mud wall with a thatched coping. The other houses of East Dean, either thatched or roofed with orange tiles, were scattered chiefly on the right.

Presently I had the willows of the river as near me on the right as the green slope, the chalk pit, the sheep-folds, and yew trees of Dean Hill on the left; and the sun shone upon the water and began to slant down the hillside. The river was very clear and swift, the chalk of its bed very white, the hair of its waving weeds very dark green.

West Dean, where I entered Wiltshire, a mile from East Dean, is a village with a " Red Lion " inn, a railway station, a sawmill and timber-yard, and several groups of houses clustering close to both banks of the river, which is crossed by a road-bridge and by a white footbridge below. I went over river and railway uphill past the new but ivied church to look at the old farm-house, the old church, and the camp, which lie back from the

road on the left among oaks and thickets. On
that Sunday morning cows pasturing on the rushy
fields below the camp, and thrushes singing in the
oaks, were the principal inhabitants of West Dean.
I did not go farther in this direction, for the road
went north to West Tytherley and the broad woods
that lie east of it, the remnant of Buckholt Forest,
but turned back and west, and then south-west
again on my original road, in order to be on the
road nearest to Dean Hill. This took me over
broad and almost hedgeless fields, and through a
short disconnected fragment of an avenue of mossy-
rooted beeches, to West Dean Farm. Nothing lay
between the houseless road and the hillside, which
is thick here with yew, except the broad arable
fields, with a square or two given up to mustard
flowers and sheep, and West Dean Farm itself. It
is a house of a dirty white colour amidst numerous
and roomy outbuildings, thatched or mellow-tiled,
set in a circle of tall beeches. The road bends round
the farm group and goes straight to the foot of the
hill, and then along it. I went slowly, looking up
at the yews and thorns on the green wall of the hill,
and its slanting green trackway, and the fir trees
upon the ridge. Linnets twittered in companies
or sang solitarily on thorn tips. Thrushes sang in
the wayside yews. Larks rose and fell unceasingly.

The sheep-bells tinkled in the mustard. Away from the hill the land sloped gradually in immense arable fields, and immense grass fields newly rolled into pale green stripes, down to the river, and there rose again up to Hound Wood and Bentley Wood, where a white house shone pale in the north-east, four or five miles off.

For nearly two miles the road had not had a house upon it, and nothing separated me from the hill, the yew trees, and the brier and hawthorn thickets. In fact, West Dean Farm was the only house served by the three miles of road between West Dean and West Grimstead. Yet this did not save a chalk pit close to the road from being used as a receptacle for rubbish. Having reached the farm and the foot of the hill the road began to turn away again towards the river and to West Grimstead. It was a loose, flinty road, so that I had another reason for walking instead of riding. The larks that sang over me could not have wished for better dust baths than this road would make them, for the sun was gaining. It was almost a treeless road until I was close to West Grimstead, where there was an oak wood on the right, streaked with the silver of birch stems and tipped with the yellow flames of larches. The village consisted of a church, an inn called the " Spring Cottage," and

many thatched cottages scattered along several
by-roads on either side. It ended in an old thatched
cottage with outbuildings, at the verge of a deep
sand pit full of sand-martins' holes. When I had
passed it I stopped at a gate and looked at the orange
pit wall on the far side, the cottage above the wall,
and the elm between the road and the pit. A
thrush and several larks were singing, and through
their songs I heard a thin voice that I had not heard
for six months, very faint yet unmistakable,
though I could not at once see the bird—a sand-
martin. I recognized the sound, as I always recognize at their first autumnal ascent above the
horizon the dim small cluster of the Pleiades on a
September evening. On such a morning one sand-
martin seems enough to make a summer, and here
were six, flitting in narrow circles like butterflies
with birds' voices.

I went on and found myself in a flat land of oak
woods and of fields that were half molehills and half
rushes, and the hedge banks had gorse in blossom.
It was here that I joined the Southampton and
Salisbury road, a yellow road between the gorsy,
rolling fragments of Whaddon Common, which
came to an end at a plantation of pines on and
about some mounds like tumuli on the right hand.

Uphill to Alderbury I walked, looking back

south-eastward along the four-mile wall of Dean
Hill which I had quitted a mile behind. Alderbury,
its " Green Dragon," its public seat and foursquare
fountain of good water for man and beast (erected
by Jacob, sixth Earl of Radnor), is on a hilltop over-
looking the Avon, and immediately on leaving it I
began to descend and to slant nearer and nearer the
river. The hedges of the road guided my eyes
straight to the cathedral spire of Salisbury, two
or three miles off beneath me. On the right the
sward and oaks of Ivychurch came down to the road :
below on the left the sward was wider, the oaks
were fewer, and many cows were feeding. A long
cleft of rushy turf and oaks, then a broad ploughland
succeeded the Ivychurch oaks, and the ploughland
rose up into a round summit crested by a clump of
pines and beeches. I remember seeing this field
when it was being ploughed by two horses, and the
ploughman's white dog was exploring on one side
or another across the slopes.

Over beyond the river the land swelled up into
chalk hills, here smooth and green, with a clump on
the ridge, and there wooded. The railway was now
approaching the road from the right, and the
narrow strip between road and railway was occupied
by an old orchard and a large green chestnut tree.
In the branches of the chestnut sang a chaffinch,

while a boy was trimming swedes underneath. I was now at the suburban edge of Salisbury, the villas looking out of their trees and lemon-coloured barberry at the double stream of Avon, at the willowy marshland, the cathedral, and the Harnham Down racecourse above.

I crossed over Harnham bridge where the tiled roofs are so mossy, and went up under that bank of sombre-shimmering ivy just to look from where the roads branch to Downston, Blandford, and Odstock. Southward nothing is to be seen except the workhouse and the many miles of bare down and sheepfolds. Northward the cathedral spire soars out of a city without a hill, dominated on the right or east by Burroughs Hill, a low but decided bluff, behind which are the broad woods of Clarendon. The road was deserted. It was on a Tuesday evening, after market, that I had last been there, when clergy with wives and daughters were cycling out past a wagon for Downton drawn by horses with red and blue plumelets; motor cyclists were tearing in; a tramp or two trudged down towards the bridge. In the city itself the cattle were being driven to the slaughter-house or out to the country, a spotted calf was prancing on the pavement, one was departing for Wilton in a crowded motor bus, a wet, new-born one stood in a cart with its mother,

a cow with udders wagging was being hustled up the
Exeter road by motor cars and pursued at a distance
by a man who called to it affectionately as a last
resource; another calf was being held outside a
pub. while the farmer drank; black and white pigs
were steered cautiously past plate glass; and in the
market-place Sidney Herbert and Henry Fawcett
on their pedestals were looking out over the dark,
wet square at the last drovers and men in gaiters
leaving it, and ordinary passengers crossing it, and
a few sheep still bleating in a pen. And the green
river meadows and their elms and willows chilled
and darkened as the gold sun sank without staining
the high, pale-washed sky, and the cathedral clock
nervously and quietly said, "One-two, one-two,
one-two" for the third quarter before dark.

But this was Sunday morning, and still early. I
ate breakfast to the tune of the "Marseillaise,"
sung slowly and softly to a child as a lullaby,
and was soon out again, this time amidst jackdaws, rooks, clergy, and the black-dressed Sunday
procession, diversified by women in violet, green,
and curry colour. The streets, being shuttered and
curtained, robbed of the crowd shopping, were cold
and naked; even the inns of Salisbury, whose
names are so genial and succulent—"Haunch of
Venison," "Round of Beef," "Ox," "Royal

George," "Roebuck," "Wool Pack"—were as near as possible dismal. Their names were as meaningless as those of the dead Browns, Dowdings, Burtons, Burdens, and Fullfords in St. Edmund's Churchyard. If it had not been for the women it would have been a city of the dead or a city of birds. The people kept to the paths of the close. The lawns and trees were given over exclusively to the birds, especially those that are black, such as the rook and blackbird. Those that were not matrimonially engaged on the grass were cawing in the elms, beeches, and chestnuts of the cathedral. Missel-thrushes were singing across the close as if it had been empty. A lark from the fields without drifted singing over the city. The stock-doves cooed among the carved saints. There were more birds than men in Salisbury. Never had I seen the cathedral more beautiful. The simple form of the whole must have been struck out of glaucous rock at one divine stroke. If seemed to belong to the birds that flew about it and lodged so naturally in the high places. The men who crawled in at the doors, as into mines, could not be the masters of such a vision.

Nevertheless, I took the liberty of entering myself, chiefly to look again for those figures of Death and a Traveller, where the Traveller says,—

> " Alas, Death, alas, a blissful thing that were
> If thou wouldst spare us in our lustiness
> And come to wretches that be so of heavy cheer." . . .

and Death retorts,—

> " Graceless gallant, in all thy lust and pride,
> Remember that thou shalt give due.
> Death shall from thy body thy soul divide.
> Thou must not him escape certainly.
> To the dead bodies cast down thine eye,
> Behold them well, consider and see,
> For such as they are such shalt thou be."

There is little more to be said about death than
is said here. But I could not find the words,
though I went up and down those streets of knights',
ladies', and doctors' tombs, and saw again old
Eleonor Sadler, grim, black, and religious, kneeling at her book in a niche since 1622, and looking
as if she could have been the devil to those who
did not do likewise. I saw, too, the tablet of Henry
Hele, who practised medicine felicitously and hon-
ourably, for fifty years, in the close and in the
city ; and the green lady with the draped harp
mourning over Thomas, Baron Wyndham, Lord
High Steward of Ireland (1681–1745), and the bust
of Richard Jefferies,—

> " Who, observing the works of Almighty God
> With a poet's eye, | Has |
> enriched the literature of his country, | and |
> won for himself a place amongst | those |
> who have made men happier, | and wiser."

If Jefferies had to be commemorated in a cathedral, it was unnecessary to drag in Almighty God. Perhaps the commemorator hoped thus to cast a halo over the man and his books; but I think " The Story of my Heart " and " Hours of Spring " will be proof against the holy water of these feeble and ill divided words.

Outside the city I had the road to Wilton, a road lined on both sides by elms, almost to myself. The rooks cawed in their nests in the elms, and the eight bells of Bemerton called to worshippers from among the trees, a field's-breadth distant on the left.   I was not tempted by the bells, yet this was one of those Sundays that help us to see beauty and a sort of sense in the lines of George Herbert, vicar of Bemerton,—

> " Sundays the pillars are
> On which heav'ns palace arched lies :
> The other days fill up the spare
> And hollow room with vanities.
> They are the fruitful beds and borders
> In God's rich garden : that is bare
>   Which parts their ranks and orders.
>   The Sundays of man's life,
> Threaded together on time's string,
> Make bracelets to adorn the wife
> Of the eternal, glorious King.
> On Sundays heaven's gate stands ope ;
> Blessings are plentiful and rife,
>   More plentiful than hope."

Izaak Walton says that on the Sunday before his
death Herbert rose up suddenly from his bed,
called for one of his instruments, tuned it, and sang
this verse: " Thus he sung on earth such hymns
and anthems as the angels and he . . . now sing
in Heaven." The bells, the sunshine after storm,
the elm trees, and the memory of that pious poet,
put me into what was perhaps an unconscious
imitation of a religious humour.   And in that
humour, repeating the verses with a not wholly
sham unction, I rode away from Bemerton.
The Other Man, however, overtook me, and upset
the humour. For he repeated in his turn, with
unction exaggerated to an incredibly ridiculous
degree, the sonnet on Sin which comes next to
that on Nature in Herbert's " Temple,"—

> " Lord, with what care hast thou begirt us round.
> Parents first season us : then schoolmasters
> Deliver us to laws ; they send us bound
> To rules of reason, holy messengers,
> Pulpits and Sundays, sorrow dogging sin,
> Afflictions sorted, anguish of all sizes,
> Fine nets and stratagems to catch us in,
> Bibles laid open, millions of surprises,
> Blessings beforehand, ties of gratefulness,
> The sound of glory ringing in our ears :
> Without, our shame ; within, our consciences ;
> Angels and grace, eternal hopes and fears.
> Yet all these fences and their whole array
> One cunning bosom-sin blows quite away."

At the conclusion of this, without pause or change of tone, he continued : " From Parents, School-masters, and Parsons, from Sundays and Bibles, from the Sound of Glory ringing in our ears, from Shame and Conscience, from Angels, Grace, and Eternal Hopes and Fears, Good Lord, or whatever Gods there be, deliver us." This so elated him that he rode on at a great pace, and I lost him. For I dismounted at Fugglestone St. Peter, a very small, short-spired church with its churchyard, huddled into a narrow wayside patch. Church and churchyard are usually locked, so that you must get over the wall, if you wish to walk about on the shaven turf amongst ivy and periwinkle · and the headstones of the Wiltshires, Bennetts, Lakes, Tabors, and Hollys, and to see middle-aged George Williams's uncomfortable words (in 1842),—

> " Dangers stand thick through all the ground
>   To push us to the tomb,
>   And fierce diseases wait around
>   To hurry mortals home."

and J. Harris's double-edged epitaph (1793),—

> " How strangely fond of life poor mortals be,
>   How few that see our beds would change with we.
>   But, serious reader, tell me which is best,
>   The painful journey or the traveller's rest ? "

Harris was trying to imagine what it would be like, lying there in Fugglestone Churchyard, and having the laugh of people who were still perpendicular; but, of course, it is most likely that Harris never wrote it.

I did not go into Wilton, but kept on steadily alongside the Wylye. For three miles I had on my left hand the river and its meadows, poplars, willows, and elms—the railway raised slightly above the farther bank—and the waved green wall of down beyond, to the edge of which came the dark trees of Grovely. It was such another scene as the Wey and the natural terrace west of Farnham. The road was heavy and wet, being hardly above the river level, but that was all the better for seeing the maidenhair lacework of the greening willows, the cattle among the marsh-marigolds of the flat green meadows, the moorhen hurried down the swift water, the bulging wagons of straw going up a deep lane to the sheepfolds, and the gradual slope of the Plain where those sheepfolds were, on my right. This edge of the Plain above the Wylye is a beautiful low downland, cloven by coombs and topped by beech clumps; and where it was arable the flints washed by last night's rain were shining in the sun. A few motor cyclists, determined men, passed me at twenty miles an hour through South Newton. Larks sang high, and hedge-sparrows sang low.

This was a great hare country, as I knew by two
tokens. When I had last come to South Newton
a band of shooters, retrievers, and beaters was
breaking up. A trap weighted with two ordinary
men and a polished, crimson-faced god of enormous
size drove off. Lord Pembroke's cart followed,
full of dead hares. . . . Some years before that I
was on Crouch's Down, on the other side of Grovely
Wood, enjoying the green road which runs between
the ridge and the modern highroad. It was open
land, with some arable below, the Grovely oaks
and their nightingales above, and the spire of Salisbury far off before me. Out of a warm, soft sky
descended a light whisking rain, and on the Down
seven hares were playing follow-my-leader at full
speed. All seven ran in a bunch round and round,
sometimes encircling a grass tussock in rings so
very small at times that only they knew which was
leader. Suddenly one leaped out of this ring, and
all pursued him in a long, open string like hounds.
Several times this happened. For twenty, fifty,
or a hundred yards they ran straight; then they
turned suddenly back almost on their own traces,
in the same open order, until their fancy preferred
circles or zigzags. Again they set off on a long
race towards a hillside beech clump, going down a
cleft above Baverstock. They made a dozen sharp

turns in the cleft, always at full speed. Maintaining the same long drawn out line, they next made for the woods above. In this long run the line opened out still more, but no one gave up. They entered the woods, to reappear immediately one at a time, and took once more to encircling a tussock. As they were usually two hundred yards away on downland of nearly their own colour, I could not be sure how often they changed their leader, but I think they did at least once in mid-career. They were as swift and happy as birds, and made the earth seem like the air. . . .

South Newton—church, smithy, " Bell " inn, and cottages—is built mostly on the right side of the road, away from the river and its willows, which are but a few yards off. The church, of flint and stone chequer, stands a little back, the tower nearest the road, on a gentle slope of flame-shaped yews and the tombs of many Blakes. Again the road touched the river, and I looked over it to Great Wishford, its cottages and hayricks clustering about the church tower, with flag flying, and to a deep recess in the Down behind. The village has a street full of different, pretty houses, mostly built of chipped flint alternating with stone, in squares, or bands, or anyhow.

From Wishford onward the river has a good

road on either side, each with a string of villages, one or two miles apart. The " Swan " and an orange-coloured plain small house with grass and a great cedar stand at the turning which leads over the river to Great Wishford and the right bank.   I kept to the left bank, because I was about to leave the Wylye and go north up its tributary Winterbourne.   From the " Swan " I began to climb up above the river, and had a steep meadow and the farm-yard and elm trees of Little Wishford between it and me, but on my right a steep bank of elms which had less for the eye than the farther side of the river, its clean wall of down, terraced below, and the trees of Grovely peeping over.   Ahead I could see more and more of the long, broad vale of the Wylye and its willows contained within slopes, half of pasture, half arable ; and above all, the curves of the Plain flowing into and across one another.   The earth was hazy, the sky clouded, and no one who had ridden on that Good Friday and bad Saturday could have expected a fine day with any confidence.

Had I been walking, I should have turned off this road between the " Swan " and Little Wishford, on to the Plain, and so by a green road that goes high across it as far as Shrewton.   But I now kept on until the road had risen, so as to touch the edge

10

of the Plain, the arable land, the home of pewits. Here I had below me the meeting of the Wylye and Winterbourne, the thatched roofs of Stapleford scattered round it, and the road going on westward with telegraph posts along the sparse, willowy vale. I turned out of this vale at Stapleford. It is a village of many crossing roads and lanes, of houses of flint and stone chequer, in groups or isolated, under its elms and high grassy banks. The church is kept open, a clean, greenish place with Norman arches on one side, and a window illuminated by a coat of arms—a phœnix on a crown—and the words, "*Foy pour devoir.*" There are no other inscriptions. Outside I noticed the names of Goodfellow, Pavie, Barnett, Brown, Rowden, Gamlen, Leversuch. The lettering survived on the headstone of John Saph, who died in 1683, and his wife, Alice, who died in 1677.

I dipped to a withy bed, and went upstream along the Winterbourne to Berwick St. James, and as the village lies on the right bank my road took a right-angled turn by a chalk pit to cross the bridge, and another to keep its course. At first sight Berwick St. James offered an excellent dense group of cottages and farm buildings by the river, new and old thatched roofs, and walls of flint or of black boarding. The church tower peered up on the right, with a mill

bestriding the stream : on the left a white house
and blossoming fruit trees stood somewhat apart
in their enclosure of white mud wall.   The sky over
all was dim, the thin white clouds showing the blue
behind them.   The street ending in the " Boot "
inn was a perfect neat one of flint and stone chequer
and thatch.   The church is kept locked.   It was open
at that moment, but occupied.   Its broad tower,
which is at the road end, is almost as broad as itself.
It has a gray, weedy churchyard, far too large for
the few big ivy-covered box tombs lying about in
it like unclaimed luggage on a railway platform.

The Winterbourne guides you through the heart
of the Plain.   It has, I believe, no very strict
boundaries, but the Plain may be said to consist
of all that mass of downland in South Wiltshire,
which is broken only by the comparatively narrow
valleys of five rivers—the Bourn, the Avon, the
Wylye, the Nadder, and the Ebble.   Three of these
valleys, however, those of the Bourn on the east,
and of the Wylye and the Nadder on the south,
have railways in them as well as rivers.   The railways are more serious interruptions to the character of the Plain, and whether or not they must
be regarded as the boundaries of a reduced Plain,
certainly the core of the Plain excludes them.
Even so it has to admit the Amesbury and Mili-

tary Camp Light Railway, cutting across from the
Bourn to the Avon, and there ceasing. Within
this reduced space of fifteen by twenty miles the
Plain is nothing but the Plain. As for the military
camps, nothing may be seen of them for days
beyond the white tents gleaming in the sun like
sheep or clouds. When they are out of sight the
tumuli and ancient earthworks that abound bring
to mind more forcibly than anywhere else the fact
that, as the poet says, " the dead are more numerous
than the living."

The valleys are rivers not only of waters, but of
greenest grass and foliage. The greatest part of
the Plain is all treeless pasture, treeless arable land.
Some high places, as at meetings of roads, possess
beeches or fir trees in line or cluster. Where the
ground falls too steeply for cultivation a copse
has been formed—a copse in one case, between
Shrewton and Tilshead, of beautiful contour, following the steep wall of chalk for a quarter of a mile
in a crescent curve, with level green at its foot,
the high Down rising bare above it. A space here
and there has been left to thorns and gorse bushes.
In several places, as at Asserton Farm above Berwick
St. James, plantations have been made in mathe-
matical forms. But as you travel across the Plain
you come rarely to a spot where the chief thing

for the eye is not an immense expanse of the colour
of ploughed chalkland, or of corn, or of turf, vary-
ing according to season and weather, and always
diversified by parallelograms of mustard yellow.
Sometimes this expanse rolls but little before it
touches the horizon; far more often, it heaves
or billows up boldly into several long curving ridges
that intersect or flow into one another. The
highest of these may be crowned by dark beeches
or carved by the ditch and rampart of an ancient
camp. Hedges are few, even by the roads. The
roads are among the noblest, visiting the rivers and
their orchards and thatched villages, but keeping
for the main part of their length high and dry and
in long curves. They are travelled by an occasional (but not sufficiently occasional) motor car,
or by a homeward going farm-roller with children
riding the horses.

Next to the dead the most numerous things on
the Plain are sheep, rooks, pewits, and larks. To-
day they mingle their voices, but the lark is the
most constant. Here, more than elsewhere, he
rises up above an earth only less free than the
heavens. The pewit is equally characteristic. His
Winter and twilight cry expresses for most men both
the sadness and the wildness of these solitudes.
When his Spring cry breaks every now and then,

as it does to-day, through the songs of the larks,
when the rooks caw in low flight or perched on their
elm tops, and the lambs bleat, and the sun shines,
and the couch fires burn well, and the wind blows
their smoke about, the Plain is genial, and the un-
kindly breadth and simplicity of the scene in Winter
or in the drought of Summer are forgotten. But
let the rain fall and the wind whirl it, or let the sun
shine too mightily, the Plain assumes the character by which it is best known, that of a sublime,
inhospitable wilderness. It makes us feel the age
of the earth, the greatness of Time, Space, and
Nature; the littleness of man even in an aeroplane,
the fact that the earth does not belong to man, but
man to the earth. And this feeling, or some variety
of it, for most men is accompanied by melancholy,
or is held to be the same thing. This is perhaps
particularly so with townsmen, and above all with
writers, because melancholy is the mood most easily
given an appearance of profundity, and, therefore,
most easily impressive.

The Plain has not attracted many writers, though
in the last few years have appeared Miss Ella Noyes's
careful collection of notes and observations, and
Mr. W. H. Hudson's "Shepherd's Life," the best
book on the Plain, one of the best of all country
books, and one that lacks all trace of writer's

melancholy.   John Aubrey wrote one or two of his
casual immortal pages on it.   Drayton called it the
first of Plains, and gave some reasons for it in his
great poem on this renowned isle of Great Britain.
Hundreds of archæologists have linked themselves
to it in libraries.   But the most famous book in
some way connected with it is Sir Philip Sidney's
"Arcadia."   Perhaps this is one of those famous
books which are never buried because the funeral
expenses would be too large, though much still remains
to be done before we shall know, as we should like
to know, why and how " Arcadia " and similar books
appealed to the men and women of England from
1590 to 1630, during which ten editions were called
for ; what kind of truth and beauty they saw in it ;
what part of their humanity was moved by it ;
whether they detected the influence of Wilton and
Salisbury Plain. . . .

Our own attitude towards it is not so hard to
explain.   That it is called " Arcadia " and is by
Sidney is something, and in these days of docile
antiquarian taste it may be enough for the few
or many who read it first in the most recent edi-
tion, the third issued during the last century and
a half.   I doubt whether even these will do more
than dream and doze and wake, lazily turning
over page after page—nearly seven hundred pages

of painfully small type—without ever making out
the plot, often forgetting who is the speaker, where
the scene, only for the sake of the most famous
passage of all,—

" There were hills which garnished their proud
heights with stately trees ; humble valleys whose
base estate seemed comforted with the refreshing of
silver rivers ; meadows enamelled with all sorts of
eye-pleasing flowers ; thickets which, being lined
with most pleasant shade, were witnessed so too
by the cheerful disposition of many well-tuned
birds ; each pasture stored with sheep feeding with
sober security, while the pretty lambs with bleating oratory craved the dams' comfort ; here a
shepherd's boy piping, as though he never should
be old ; there a young shepherdess knitting, and
withal singing, and it seemed that her voice comforted her hands to work, and her hands kept
time to her voice-music." . . .

(A charming companion to this first view of Arcadia is where FitzGerald speaks of the home-
brewed at Yardley, in the days before " he knew
he was to die.") For a page or two the least
learned of us can enjoy the ghostly rustle of these
vaporous, eloquent forms that never were alive, yet
once gave joy to men who were friends of Shakespeare and Drake ; the phantoms of their felicity

in gardens and fair women. Then the beauty of
visible things, of dress, for example, abounds and is
very real, especially Pyrocles' dress in his Amazon's
disguise—the hair arrayed in " careless care " under
a coronet of pearl and gold and feathers, the doub-
let " of sky-coloured satin, with plates of gold, and,
as it were, nailed with precious stones." The
princeliness of the Arcadians' manners and morals
may seem to reflect Sidney's self " divinely mild,
a spirit without spot." There are thoughts, too,
beyond such as the convention demanded, as when
Pyrocles says,—

" I am not yet come to that degree of wisdom
to think light of the sex of whom I have my life,
since if I be anything, which your friendship rather
finds than I acknowledge, I was, to come to it, born
of a woman, nursed of a woman. . . . Truly we men,
and praisers of men, should remember that if we
have such excellences it is reasonable to think
them excellent creatures, of whom we are—since a
kite never brought forth a good flying hawk."
And some of the situations, conventional enough,
only the weary or those that never loved can pass
unsaluted ; such as Amphialus' too felicitous court-
ship of Queen Helen on behalf of his foster-brother,
Philoxenos. The conceits, too, do not tower so
often, so bravely, so rashly, into the cloudy alti-

tudes without meeting what would not have been
found at home : as in Kalander's hunting,—

" The wood seemed to conspire with them against
his own citizens [that is, the stags], dispersing their
noise through all his quarters, and even the nymph
left to bewail the loss of Narcissus and became a
hunter."

The nymphs themselves, enchanted by the
pleasant ways of the pastoral, are sometimes
lured out of their fastnesses to bless it with a
touch of eternal Nature or of true rusticity, as in the
Eclogue in the third book : " The first strawberries
he could find, were ever in a clean washed dish
sent to Kala; thus posies of the spring flowers
were wrapped up in a little green silk, and dedi-
cated to Kala's breasts; thus sometimes his
sweetest cream, sometimes the best cake-bread
his mother made, were reserved for Kala's taste.
Neither would he stick to kill a lamb when she
would be content to come over the way unto
him."

Delightful, too, is the use of experience when it
is said of Pyrocles that his mind was " all this while
so fixed upon another devotion, that he no more
attentively marked his friend's discourse than the
child that hath leave to play marks the last part
of his lesson."

This has nothing to do with the Plain. We
know, indeed, that Sidney wrote it below there at
Wilton, in his sister, the Countess of Pembroke's
house. But what has "Arcadia" to do with
Wilton, save that it was written there? There,
says Aubrey, the Muses appeared to Sidney, and
he wrote down their dictates in a book, even
though on horseback. " These romancy plaines
and boscages did no doubt," says he, a Wiltshire
man, " conduce to the heightening of Sir Philip
Sidney's phansie." It cannot be said that they
did more, that they reflected themselves in the
broad, meandering current of the " Arcadia." At
most, perhaps, after heightening the poet's fancy,
they offered no impediments to it. If Salisbury
Plain was not Arcadia, it contained the elements of
Arcadia and a solitude in which they could be
mingled at liberty. Every one must wish for a
larger leaven of passages like that one where he
compares Pyrocles to the impatient schoolboy, for
something to show us what he and the countess said
and did at Wilton, and what the Plain was like,
three hundred years ago, when the book was being
written. Even so it is a better preparation for
Salisbury Plain than it would be for Sedgemoor or
Land's End; but I shall not labour the point
since I had seen the Plain before I had read the

book, and Berwick St. James is as little affected by
" Arcadia " as " Arcadia " by Berwick St. James.

As soon as my road was outside Berwick St.
James it mounted above the river and was absolutely clear of houses, hedges, and fences for a
mile, and showed me nothing more than the bare
and the green arable land flowing away on every
side in curves like flight, and compact masses of
beeches on certain ridges, like manes or combs.
At the end of the mile my northward road ran
into a westward road from Amesbury, turned sharp
along it for a hundred yards or so, and then out
of it sharp to the left and north again, thus seeing
nothing of the village of Winterbourne Stoke but
a group of sycamores and a thatched white mud
wall round which it twisted.   Out and up the road
took me again to the high arable without a hedge,
and the music of larks, and the mingling sounds of
pewits and sheep-bells.   Before me scurried par-
tridges, scarce willing to give up their love-making
in the sunlit and sun-warmed dust.   Looking over
my shoulder I saw two hills striped with corn,
and one of them crested with beeches, curve up
apart from one another, so as to frame in the
angle thus made between them the bare flank of
Berwick Down and the outline of Yarnbury Castle
ramparts upon the bare ridge of it.   Very far

northward hung the dark-wooded inland promon-
tory of Martinsell, near Savernake, and in the east
the Quarley and Figsbury range, their bony humps
just tipped with dark trees.

The next village was five villages in one—Rolle-
stone, Maddington, Shrewton, Orcheston St. George,
and Orcheston St. Mary. Here many roads from
the high land descended to the river and crossed
mine. The cluster of villages begins with orchard
and ends in a field where the grass is said to grow
twelve feet high. After passing over the Winterbourne and running along under its willows to
Shrewton's little domed dungeon of blackened stone,
and an inn that stands sideways to the road, with
the sign of a Catherine-wheel, the road again
bridges the river from waterside Shrewton to
waterside Maddington. But I kept along the
Shrewton bank on a by-road. The stream here
flows as clear as glass over its tins and crockery,
between roadside willows and a white mud wall,
and I followed it round past the flint-towered
church and the " Plume of Feathers " and its pair
of peacock yews. I was looking for Orcheston St.
Mary. One sunny February day, when the fields
by the road hither from Tilshead were flooded with
pools and channels of green, peacock blue, and purple
by the Winterbourne, I had seen below me among

the loops of the water a tiny low-towered church
with roof stained orange, and a white wall curving
and long, and a protective group of elms, which was
Orcheston St. Mary.   I continued along the stream
and its banks of parsley and celandine, its troop of
willows, beeches, and elms, but found myself at
Orcheston St. George.   A cottage near the church
bore upon its wall these words, cut in stone, before
Queen Victoria's time,—

> "Fear God
> Honour the King
> Do good to all men."

Probably it dates from about the year of Alton
Workhouse, from the times when kites and ravens
abounded, and thrived on the corpses of men who
were hanged for a little theft committed out of
necessity or love of sport.   The fear of God must
have been a mighty thing to bring forth such
laws and still more the obedience to them.   And
yet, thanks to our capacity for seeing the past and
the remote in rose-colour, that age frequently
appears as at least a silver age; perhaps even our
own will appear German silver.   I confess I did
not think about the lad who was hanged for a hare
when I caught sight of the church at Orcheston
St. George, but rather of some imaginary, blissful
time which at least lacked our tortures, our great

men, our shame and conscience. It is a flint
church with an ivied tower standing on terms
of equality among thatched farm buildings and
elms. The church was stifling, for a stove roared
among dead daffodils and moss and the bodies of
Ambrose Paradice, gent, dead since 1727, and Joan
his wife, and the mere tablet of John Shettler
of Elston, who died at Harnham (" from the effects
of an accident ") on December 6, 1861, when he
was fifty-two, and went to Hazelbury Brian in
Dorset to be buried. Outside, the sun was almost as
warm on the daisies and on the tombstone of Job
Gibbs, who died in 1817 at the age of sixty-four,
and proclaimed, or the sexton did for him,—

> " Ye living men the Tomb survey
> Where you must quickly dwell.
> Mark how the awful summons sounds
> In ev'ry funeral knell.
> Give joy or sorrow, care or pain,
> Take life and friends away, '
> But let me find them all again
> In that eternal day."

Close by, Ann Farr from Shropshire, a servant
for fifty years at the Rectory, had a tablet between
her and oblivion.

From Orcheston St. George the road advances
three miles with hardly a hedge. On the right
rose and spread broad pastures mainly, on the left

arable lands, new ploughed, or green with young
corn, or cut up into squares of swedes or mustard
for the long-horned sheep. There was no flooded
river now to shine in the sun. Clouds began to
thicken over the sky. The dust whirled. The
straw caught in the hawthorns fluttered. A motor
car raced by me. Therefore I did not get off my
bicycle to visit that crescent beech and fir wood
against a concavity of the chalk upon my right. A
farm road curves past it, the wood hanging above it
as beautifully as if above a river. I hoped to reach
Tilshead before it rained, or, better still, the elms
and farm buildings at Joan-a-Gore's at the crossing
of the Ridge Way. Tilshead's trees lay visible before me for a mile or more. Its street of cottages
and houses that are more than cottages I entered
before the rain. I even stopped at the church
—a flint and stone one—to see the tower and
the churchyard, and its white mud wall, and the
chestnut tree, and the ash that weeps over the box
tombs of people named Wilkins and Parham, and
the graves of the Husseys and Laweses, and that
boast of William Cowper the schoolmaster in 1804,—

> " When the Archangel's trump shall sound,
>   And slumbering mortals bid to rise,
>   I shall again my form assume
>   To meet my Saviour in the skies."

A man was just stepping out of a motor car into the " Black Horse," carrying a scarlet-hooded falcon upon his wrist; but I did not stop here, nor at the " Rose and Crown," or the " Bell."

On leaving Tilshead, as on leaving Berwick St. James, Winterbourne Stoke, and Orcheston, I was free of houses; and of the few that lay in the hollows of the Plain only one was visible—a small one on my right a quarter of a mile away among ricks and elm trees—until I came to Joan-a-Gore's. It is a hedgeless road, with more or less wide margins of rough grass, along which proceed two lines of poplars, some dead, some newly planted, all unprosperous and resembling the sails of windmills. A league of ploughland on either hand was broken only by a clump or two on the high ridges and a rick on the lower. As it was Sunday no white and black teams were crossing these spaces, sowing or scarifying. The rooks of Joan-a-Gore's flew back and forth, ignorant of the falconer; the pewit brandished himself in the air; the lark sang continually; on one of the dead poplars a corn bunting delivered his unvaried song, as if a handful of small pebbles dropped in a chain dispiritedly. Nobody was on the road, it being then two o'clock, except a young soldier going to meet a girl. The rain came, but was gone again before

11

I reached Joan-a-Gore's. The farm-house, the spacious farm-yard and group of irregular, shadowy, thatched buildings, and the surrounding rookery elms, all on a gently-sloping ground next to the road—this is the finest modern thing on the Plain. The farm itself is but a small, slated house, gray-white in colour, with a porch and five front windows, half hid among elm trees; but the whole group probably resembles a Saxon chief's homestead. The trees make a nearly continuous copse with the elms and ashes that stand around and above the thatched cart lodges and combined sheds and cottages at Joan-a-Gore's Cross. No hedge, wall, or fence divides this group from my road or from the Ridge Way crossing it, and I turned into one of the doorless cart lodges to eat. I sat on a wagon shaft, looking out north over the Ridge Way and the north edge of the Plain. Where it passed the cart lodge the Ridge Way was a dusty farm track; but on the other side of the crossing it was a fair road, leading past a new farm group towards Imber. Chickens pecked round me in the road dust and within the shed. Sparrows chattered in the thatch. The bells of sheep folded in neighbouring root fields tinkled. In the rookery the rooks cawed, and nothing intimated that the falcon had killed one. The young soldier had met his girl, and was walking back with her hand in his. The heavy dark sagging clouds let out some rain without silencing the larks. As the sun came out again a trapful of friends of the cottagers drove up. The trap was drawn up alongside of me with a few stares : the women went in; the men put away the horse and strolled about. Well, I could not rest here when I had finished eating. Perhaps Sunday had tainted the solitude and quiet; I know not. So I mounted and rode on north-westward.

The road was beginning to descend off the Plain. The poplars having come to an end, elms lined it on both sides. When the descent steepened the road-side banks became high and covered in arum, parsley, nettle, and ground ivy, and sometimes elder and ivy. No hedgerow on the left hid the great waves of the Plain towards Imber, and the fascinating hollow of the Warren close at hand. The slabby ploughland sinks away to a sharp-cut, flat-bottomed hollow of an oblong tendency, enclosed by half-wooded, green terraced banks all round except at the entrance, which is towards the road. This is the Warren, a most pleasant thing to see, a natural theatre unconsciously improved by human work, but impossible to imitate entirely by art, and all the better for being empty.

Nearing the foot of the descent the road on the

left is blinded by a fence, so that I could hardly
see the deep wooded cleave parallel to me, and
could only hear the little river running down it
to Lavington. Very clear and thin and bright
went this water over the white and dark stones
by the wayside, as I came down to the forge at
West Lavington and the " Bridge " inn. West
Lavington is a street of about two miles of cottages, a timber-yard, inns, a great house, a church,
and gardens, with interruptions from fields. All
Saints' Church stands upon a steep bank on the
left, a towered church with a staircase corner
turret and an Easter flag flying. Round about it
throng the portly box tombs and their attendant
headstones, in memory of the Meads, Saunderses,
Bartlets, Naishes, Webbs, Browns, Allens, and the
rest. Among the Browns is James Brown, shepherd " for thirty-nine years," who died in 1887,
and was then but forty-six. The trees and thatched
and tiled roofs of the village hid the Plain from
the churchyard. Inside, the church wall was well
lined with tablets to the Tinkers, the Smiths, and
the family of Amor ; but the principal thing is
the recumbent marble figure of Henry Danvers,
twenty-one years old when he died in 1654. He
is musing over a book which appears to be slipping
from his grasp. The figure of his mother, Eliza-

beth, near him is also holding but not reading a
book. Between the two an earlier female effigy, head
on cushion, slumbers in a recess. Under one of the
largest tablets a tiny stone with quaint lettering
was inset to keep in mind Henevera Yerbury, who
died at Coulston on March 4, 1672.

Instead of going straight on through Potterne
and Devizes, I turned to the left by the Dauntsey
Agricultural College, and entered a road which follows the foot of the Plain westward to Westbury
and Frome. Thus I had the north wall of the Plain
always visible on my left as I rode through Little
Cheverell, Erlestoke, Tinhead, and Edington. The
road twisted steeply downhill between high banks of
loose earth and elm roots, half draped by arum,
dandelion, ground ivy, and parsley, and the flowers
of speedwell and deadnettle; then up again to
Little Cheverell. Here I mounted a bank of
nettles and celandines under elm trees into the
churchyard, and between two pairs of pollard limes
to the door of the church, and walked round it and
saw the two box tombs smothered in ivy, and the
spotted old carved stones only two feet out of the
ground. Behind the church rises Strawberry Hill.
A cow was lowing in the farmyard over the road.
Fowls were scratching deeper and deeper the holes
among the elm roots on the church bank.

Then for a distance the road traversed hedgeless arable levels that rose gently in their young green garments up to the Plain. I looked back, and saw the vast wall of the Plain making an elbow at West Lavington, and crooking round to a clump on a straw-coloured hill above Urchfont, the farthest point visible. Before me stretched the woods of Erlestoke Park, crossing the road and slanting narrow and irregular up and along the hillside, lining it with beech and fir for over a mile, under the name of Hill Wood. The road dipped steeply through the grounds of the park, and its high banks of gray sand, dressed in dog's mercury and ivy, and overhung by pine trees, shut out everything on either hand. Several private bridges crossed the deep road, and a woman had stopped that her child might shout, " Cuckoo! Cuckoo! " under the arch of one of them. Emerging from these walls, the road cut through a chain of ponds. Erlestoke Park lay on both sides. On the right its deer fed by the new church under a steep rise of elms and sycamores; on the left rooks cawed among the elms and chestnuts scattered on lawn that sloped up to Hill Wood.

A timber-yard, a "George and Dragon," and many neat thatched cottages compose the wayside village of Erlestoke. Water was flashing down the gutters.

Quite a number of people were on the road, but no one could tell me the meaning of the statuary niched on the cottage walls. It must have come from " some old ancient place," they said. An old man who had dwelt for eighteen years in one of the cottages thus adorned, and had worked as a boy with old men that knew the place, could tell me no more. Some of the figures were nudes—one a female, with the coy hands of Venus, rising from her bath—others classical, and symbolic or grotesque: all astonishing in that position, ten feet up on a cottage wall, and unlikely to have come from the old church in Erlestoke Park.

Not a mile of this road was without cottagers strolling with their children or walking out to see friends in the beautiful weather. But just outside Erlestoke I met two slightly dilapidated women, not cottage women, with a perambulator, and twenty yards behind them two weatherbeaten, ablebodied men in caps, better dressed than the women. As I went by, one of them gave a shout, which I did not take as meant for me. He continued to shout what I discovered to be " Sir " in a loud voice until I turned round and had to get down. They advanced to meet me. The shorter man, a stocky fellow of not much past thirty, with very little nose, thin lips, and a strong, shaven chin, hastened up to me and inquired, in an unnecessarily decided manner, the road to Devizes, and if there were many houses on the way. The taller man, slender and very upright, with bright blue eyes, had by this time come up, and the two began to beg, telling rapidly, loudly, emphatically, and complainingly, a combined story into which the *Titanic* was introduced. One of them pointed out that he was wearing the button of the Seamen's Guild. They wanted me to look at papers. The two women, who were still walking on, they claimed as their wives. The more they talked the less inclined did I feel to give them money. Though they began to call down a blessing on me, I still refused. They persisted. The shorter one was not silent while I mounted my bicycle. So I rode away out of reach of their blessings without giving them anything. I tried to explain to myself why. For sixpence I might have purchased two loaves or three pints for them, and for myself blessings and possibly some sort of glow. I did not know nearly enough of mankind to condemn them as mere beggars; besides, mere beggars must live, if any one must. But they were very glib and continuous. Also they were hearty men in good health—which should have been a reason for giving them what I could afford. The strongest reason against it was probably alarm at being given some responsibility at one blow for five bodies in some ways worse off than myself, and shame, too, at the act of handing money and receiving thanks for it. My conscience was uneasy. I could not appease it with sixpence, nor with half a sovereign, which might have been thought generous if I had told the story. If I was to do anything I ought to have seen the thing through, to have accompanied these people and seen that they slept dry and ate enough, and got work or a pension. To give them money was to take mean advantage of the fact that in half a mile or so I could stow them away among the mysteries and miseries of the world. Too late I concluded that I ought to have listened to their story to the end, to have read their papers and formed an opinion, and to have given what I could, because in any case I should be none the worse, and they might be the better, if only to the extent of three pints between them. I made a resolution—a sort of a resolution—to give sixpence in future to every beggar, and leave the question of right or wrong till—

> "When the Archangel's trump shall sound
> And slumbering mortals bid to rise,"

and the schoolmaster's expectation is answered. Nevertheless, I was uneasy—so uneasy that the next beggar got nothing from me. It was simpler to

pass by with a helpless " *Que sais-je ?* " shrug,
than to stop and have a look at him and say
something, while I felt in my pockets and made
the choice between my coppers and my smallest
silver.

Thus I rode up hill through more steep banks of
gray sand draped in ivy, overhung with pine trees.
Dipping again, I came to a park-like meadow, a
pond, and a small house above rather stiff, ineffectual green terraces, on my right ; while on the left
the wall of the Plain was carved from top to bottom
by three parallel even rolls like suet puddings, and
these again carved across horizontally. A little
farther on Coulston Hill was hollowed out into a
great round steep bay which had once been a
beech wood. Now all the beeches were lying anyhow, but ·mostly pointing downward, on the steep
where they had fallen or slid, some singly, some in
raft-like masses. Not a tree remained upright.
The bared, blackish earth and the gray stems—of
the colour of charred wood and ashes—suggested
fire. The disorder of the strewn debris suggested
earthquake. All was silent. A stiff man of fifty
was endeavouring to loiter without stopping still
in the road while his daughter of eighteen tried to
keep her distance behind him by picking anemones
without actually stopping.

Before Tinhead there were more vertical rolls
and corresponding troughs on the hillside, and at the
foot again three or four wide terraces, and below
them a cornfield reaching to the road. To the
low, dark-blue elm country away from the Plain—
that is, northward—and to the far wooded ridge on
its horizon, the westering light was beginning to
add a sleeplike softness of pale haze. Over the
low hedges I saw league after league of this lower
land, and the drab buttresses of Beacon Hill near
Devizes on its eastern edge. It had the appearance
of a level, uninhabitable land of many trees. Several
times a hollow cleft in the slope below the road—
a cleft walled by trees, but grass-bottomed—guides
the eye out towards it. All along good roads led
down to the vale, and an equal number of rough
roads climbed the hillside up to the Plain. I was
to go down, not up, and I looked with regret at the
clear ridge and the rampart of Bratton Castle
carved on it against the sky, the high bare
slopes, the green magnificent gulleys and horizontal
terraces, the white roads, and especially a rough
cartway mounting steeply from Edington between
prodigious naked banks. For I had formerly gone up
this cartway on a day so fine that for many nights
afterwards I could send myself to sleep by thinking of how I climbed, seeing only these precipitous

banks and the band of sky above them, until I
emerged into the glory and the peace of the Plain,
of the unbounded Plain and the unbounded sky,
and the marriage of sun and wind that was being
celebrated upon them. But it was no use going
the same way, for I was tired and alone, and it was
near the end of the afternoon, though still cloudily
bright and warm. I had to go down, not up, to
find a bed that I knew of seven or eight miles from
Tinhead and Edington.

These two are typical downside villages of brick
and thatch, built on the banks of the main road, a
parallel lane or two, and some steep connecting
lanes at right angles. When I first entered them
from below I was surprised again and again how
many steps yet higher up the downside they extended. From top to bottom the ledges and in-
clines on which they stand, and the intervening
spaces of grass and orchard, cover about half a
mile. Tinhead has an " Old George " inn of an L
shape, with a yard in the angle. Edington, almost
linked to Tinhead by cottages scattered along the
road, has a " Plough " and " Old White Horse."
They were beginning to advertise the Tinhead and
Bratton inns as suitable for teas and week-end
parties. Hence, perhaps, the prefix " Old." For
hereby is the first station since Lavington on the

line that goes parallel to the wall of the Plain and
a mile or two below the road, all along ;the Pewsey
vale to Westbury.

I turned away from the hills through Edington,
which has a big towered church among its farm-
yards, cottage gardens, and elm slopes—big enough
to seat all Edington, men and cattle.   Like Salisbury
Cathedral, this church looks as if it had been made
in one piece.   All over, it is a uniform rough gray
without ivy or moss or any stain.   On first entering the churchyard, what most struck my eye was
the name of the Rev. Hussy Cave-Browne-Cave,
for his name is on the fifth step of the cross erected
during his vicarship ; and next to that a prostrate
cross within a stone kerb, six yards long by three
yards wide, in memory of a member of the Long
family.   The church is the centre of a village of
big box tombs, some ornamented by carving, one
covered by a stone a foot thick, mossed, lichened,
stained orange and black, pitted deep by rain, and
retaining not a letter of its inscription.   I saw the
names Pike, Popler, Oram, and Fatt.   Inside, out
of the rain, lie the Longs, Carters, and Taylers, the
days of their lives conspicuously recorded, and
more than this in the case of George Tayler, since
he died in 1852, and left money for a sixpenny
cake to be given to each Sunday-school teacher,

and a threepenny one to each scholar, once a year,
" immediately after the sermon " (I think, at
Easter). Mr. Tayler was either an enemy to sermons, or did not know as much as Sir Philip Sidney
about schoolboys. One transept is the exclusive
domain of an Augustinian canon, his head on a
cushion, his feet against a barrel, while the coping-
stone of his monument is capped by a barrel and
a tree sprouting from it. The locked chancel is
peopled by effigies of great or of rich men lying
on their backs or kneeling and clasping their hands
in prayer, as they have done for centuries ; one of
them a Welshman from Glamorgan, Sir Edward
Lewys. Round about I read the names Lewis,
Price, Roberts, Phillips, and Ellis. And speaking of names, I noticed that the landlord of the
" Plough " was Pavy, a name which I had seen
at Stapleford, and long before that in the epitaph
Ben Jonson wrote on " a child of Queen Eliza-
beth's Chapel," a boy actor, Salathiel Pavy—

> " Weep with me all you that read
>   This little story ;
> And know, for whom a tear you shed,
>   Death's self is sorry.
> 'Twas a child, that so did thrive
>   In grace and feature,
> As Heaven and nature seemed to strive
>   Which owned the creature.

> Years he numbered scarce thirteen
>   When fates turned cruel ;
> Yet three filled zodiacs had he been
>   The stage's jewel ;
> And did act, what now we moan,
>   Old men so duly,
> As, sooth, the Parcæ thought him one,
>   He played so truly.
> So, by error, to his fate
>   They all consented ;
> But viewing him since, alas, too late
>   They have repented ;
> And have sought, to give new birth,
>   In baths to steep him ;
> But, being so much too good for earth,
>   Heaven vows to keep him."

The conceit and the babbling metre play most daintily with sadness ; yet I think now it would touch us little had we not a name to attach to it, the name of a boy who acted in Jonson's " Cynthia's Revels " and " Poetaster " in 1600 and 1601.

A motor car overtook me in the village, scattering a group of boys. " Look out ! " cried one, and as the thing passed by, turned to the next boy with, " There's a fine motor ; worth more than you are ; cost a lot of money." Is this not the awakening of England ? At least, it is truth. One pink foxy boy laughed in my face as if there had been iron bars or a wall of plate glass dividing us ;

another waited till I had started, to hail me, " Longlegs."

Rapidly I slid down, crossed the railway, and
found myself in a land where oaks stood in the
hedges and out in mid-meadow, and the banks
were all primroses, and a brook gurgled slow among
rush, marigold, and willow. High above me, on my
left hand, eastward, was the grandest, cliffiest part
of the Plain wall, the bastioned angle where it
bends round southward by Westbury and Warminster, bare for the most part, carved with the
White Horse and with double tiers of chalk pits,
crowned with the gigantic camps of Bratton,
Battlesbury, and Scratchbury, ploughed only on
some of the lower slopes, and pierced by the road
to Imber. The chimneys of Trowbridge made a
clump on ahead to my right. In the west the
dark ridge of the Mendips made the horizon.

I turned out of my way to see Steeple Ashton.
It has no steeple, being in fact Staple Ashton, but
a tower and a dial on a church, a very big church,
bristling with coarse crockets all over, and knobby
with coarse gargoyles, half lion and half dog, some
spewing down, some out, some up. It is not a
show village, like Lacock, where the houses are
packed as in a town, and most of the gardens
invisible ; but a happy alternation of cottages of

E.W.HASLEHUST.

stone or brick (sometimes placed herring-bone fashion) or timber work, vegetable gardens, orchard plots, and the wagon-maker's. On many a wagon for miles round the name of Steeple Ashton is painted. It is on level ground, but well up towards the Plain, over the wall of which rounded clouds, pure white and sunlit, were heaving up. Rain threatened again, but did no more. The late afternoon grew more and more quiet and still, and in the warmth I mistook a distant dog's bark, and again a cock's crowing, for the call of a cuckoo, mixed with the blackbird's singing. I strained my ears, willing to be persuaded, but was not. I was sliding easily west, accompanied by rooks going homeward, and hailed by thrushes in elm trees beside the road—through West Ashton and downhill on the straight green-bordered road between Carter's Wood and Flowery Wood. I crossed the little river Biss and went under the railway to North Bradley. This is a village built partly along the road from Westbury to Trowbridge, partly along two parallel turnings out of it. The most conspicuous houses on the main road are the red brick and stone villas with railings and small gardens, bearing the following names : The Laurels, East Lynn, Cremont, Lyndhurst, Hume Villa, Alcester Cottage, Rose Villa, and Frith House, all

12

in one row. On a dusty, cold day, when sparrows
are chattering irresolutely, this is not a cheerful
spot; nor yet when an organ-grinder is singing
and grinding at the same time, while his more
beauteous and artistic-looking mate stands de-
ceitfully by and makes all the motions but none
of the music of a baritone in pain. To the out-
ward eye, at least, the better part of North Bradley is the by-road which the old · flat-fronted
asylum of stone faces across a small green, the
church tower standing behind, half hid by trees.
I went down this road, past farms called Ireland
and Scotland on the left, and on the right a green
lane, where, among pots and pans, a gypsy cara-
van had anchored, belonging to a Loveridge of
Bristol. Venus, spiky with beams, hung in the
pale sky,· and Orion stood up before me, above
the blue woods of the horizon. All the thrushes
of England sang at that hour, and against that
background of myriads I heard two or three singing their frank, clear notes in a mad eagerness
to have all done before dark; for already the
blackbirds were chinking and shifting places
along the hedgerows. And presently it was dark,
but for a lamp at an open door, and silent, but
for a chained dog barking, and a pine tree moan-
ing over the house. When the dog ceased, an owl

hooted, and when the owl ceased I could just hear the river Frome roaring steadily over a weir far off. Before I settled into a chair I asked them what the weather was going to be like to-morrow. " Who knows ? " they said; "but we do want sun. The grass isn't looking so well as it was a month ago : it's looking browny." Had any eggs been found ? " Not one; but we've heard of them being found, and we've been looking out for plovers' eggs." I asked what they did with the song birds' eggs, and if they were ever eaten. The idea of eating such little eggs disgusted every one over fifteen; but they were fond of moorhens', and had once taken twenty-two from a single nest before the bird moved to a safe place. Yes, they had plenty of chicks, and some young ducks half grown. The turkeys were laying, but it was too early to let them sit. . . . Again I heard the weir, and I began to think of sleep.

V.

BEFORE I decided that sleep was better than
any book, some bad poetry I was reading
put me in mind of Stephen Duck. I had been
thinking of him earlier in the day at Erlestoke,
because it occurred to me that the sculpture was
as inappropriate on the cottages there as were the
frigid graces on the thresher's mortal pages. This
man, a labourer from Charlton, some way east of
Erlestoke, was made a Yeoman of the Guard in
1733 for his services to literature, and rector of
Byfleet in 1752. He drowned himself in 1755,
when he was fifty. His great achievements were,
first, to show that an agricultural labourer could
write as well as ninety-nine out of a hundred clergy-
men, gentlemen, and noblemen, and extremely
like them, for his verses rarely had more to do
with rural life than the sculpture at Erlestoke ;
second, to show, conversely, that a poet could use
a scythe, which he tells us he did—and made

" the vanquished mowers soon confess his skill "
—when revisiting his birthplace.

Instead of Stephen, George, and John, he sang
of Colin, Cuddy, and Menalcas; of Chloe and Celia,
instead of Ann and Maria. When he set himself
to write of shepherds, whom he must often have
met, it fell out thus,—

> " From Bath, I travel thro' the sultry vale,
> Till Sal'sb'ry Plains afford a cooling Gale :
> Arcadian Plains where Pan delights to dwell,
> In verdant Beauties cannot these excel :
> These too, like them, might gain immortal Fame,
> Resound with Corydon and Thyrsis' Flame ;
> If, to his Mouth, the Shepherd would apply
> His mellow Pipe, or vocal Music try."

But, alas, the poor shepherd has not heard of
pastoral poetry, and does not know—oh, happy if
his happiness he knew—that his country is Arcadia ;
for, as Duck laments,—

> " Propt on his Staff, he indolently stands ;
> His Hands support his Head, his Staff his Hands ;
> Or, idly basking in the sunny Ray,
> Supinely lazy, loiters Life away."

This is a good deal more like a poet than a
shepherd. The fellow might have retorted that
even if he converted his sheep hook into a pen he
might not be the one of whom the poet wrote,—

"Great Caroline her Royal Bounty show'd
    To one, and raised him from the grov'ling Crowd "—

that Queen Caroline could not be expected to re-
plenish the Yeomen with Arcadians only.

Duck was at least as much awed by the Queen
as by Nature. Richmond Park and the Royal
Gardens so disturbed his judgment that he believed it possible, if Pope's Muse would visit him,—

"Then Richmond Hill renown'd in Verse should grow,
    And Thames re-echo to the Song below ;
    A second Eden in my Page should shine,
    And Milton's Paradise submit to mine."

The Queen's Grotto in Richmond Gardens inspired
him with the line,—

"The sweetest Grotto and the wisest Queen."

And yet the poor man said, and in a preface published in his lifetime, " I have not myself been so
fond of writing, as might be imagined from seeing
so many things of mine as are got together in this
Book. Several of them are on Subjects that were
given me by Persons, to whom I have such great
Obligations, that I aways thought their desires
commands."

Leaving school about his fourteenth year for
" the several lowest employments of a country

life," and marrying before he was twenty, he had
to work at top pressure in order to make time to
read the *Spectator*, which he did " all over sweat
and heat, without regarding his own health." He
" got English just as we get Latin." He studied
" Paradise Lost " as others study the classics, with
the help of a dictionary. When he wrote about
the life best known to him, it was usually as any of
those gentlemen who helped him would have done.
He made very little advance on Sir Philip Sidney.

Nevertheless, some things he did write which
were true and were unlikely to have been written
by any one else, as when he described the thresher's
labour,—

> " When sooty Pease we thresh, you scarce can know
> Our native Colour as from Work we go :
> The Sweat, the Dust, and suffocating Smoke,
> Make us so much like Ethiopians look.
> We scare our Wives, when Ev'ning brings us home,
> And frighted Infants think the Bugbear come.
> Week after Week, we this dull Task pursue,
> Unless when winn'wing Days produce a new ;
> A new, indeed, but frequently a worse,
> The Threshal yields but to the Master's Curse.
> He counts the Bushels, counts how much a Day ;
> Then swears we've idled half our Time away :
> ' Why, look ye, Rogues, d'ye think that this will do ?
> Your neighbours thresh as much again as you.'
> Now in our Hands we wish our noisy Tools,
> To drown the hated Names of Rogues and Fools ;

But, wanting these, we just like Schoolboys look,
When angry Masters view the blotted Book :
They cry, ' Their Ink was faulty, and their Pen ; '
We, ' The Corn threshes bad, 'twas cut too green.' "

He might have equalled Bloomfield, he might have
been a much lesser Crabbe, if he could have thrown
Cuddy and Chloe on to the mixen and kept to the
slighted homely style. Instead of merely writing
as if he had been to Oxford, he might have reached
men's ears with his appeal,—

"Let those who feast at Ease on dainty Fare,
   Pity the Reapers, who their Feasts prepare."

As a rule his work—I mean his writing—is so
remote from Wiltshire and Duck, or the sort of
reality connected with them which we to-day look
for, that even the grain or two about Salisbury
Plain or the Pewsey Vale not quite dissolved in his
floods of Alexanderpopery delight us, as when he
calls the lambs bleating,—

"Too harsh, perhaps, to please politer Ears,
   Yet much the sweetest Tune the Farmer hears : "

or when he compares the haymakers to sparrows
at the approach of storm,—

"Thus have I seen, on a bright Summer's Day,
   On some green Brake, a Flock of Sparrows play ;

From Twig to Twig, from Bush to Bush they fly ;
And with continued Chirping fill the Sky :
But, on a sudden, if a Storm appears,
Their chirping Noise no longer dins our Ears.
They fly for Shelter to the thickest Bush,
There silent sit, and all at once is hush."

He says little more than enough to make us feel
how much he could have said if—well, if, for
example, he had been the sort of man to wish to
employ his flail, not to drown the master's curses,
but to break his head. But he was ineffectual, if
not beautiful. The only known material effect of
his verse was to draw charity from Lord Palmerston
for providing an annual threshers' dinner, which is
still given at Charlton on June 30. This feast
proves him greater as prophet than as poet in
writing,—

" Oft as this Day returns, shall Temple cheer
The Threshers' Hearts with Mutton, Beef, and Beer ;
Hence, when their Children's Children shall admire
This Holiday, and, whence deriv'd, inquire,
Some grateful Father, partial to my Fame,
Shall thus describe from whence, and how it came :
' Here, Child, a Thresher liv'd in ancient Days ;
Quaint Songs he sung, and pleasing Roundelays ;
A gracious Queen his Sonnets did commend,
And some great Lord, one Temple, was his Friend.
That Lord was pleas'd this Holiday to make,
And feast the Threshers for that Thresher's sake.' "

A hundred years were.to pass before a countryman came to do something of what Duck left
undone, but, however honestly, did it from the
point of view of a spectator, a clergyman, a schoolmaster, an archæologist, a reader of Tennyson,
and the refined contemplators of rural life. He
lived and died in a country of which most of
the conditions are to be paralleled on Salisbury
Plain and the Pewsey Vale. I mean William
Barnes.

Dorset is a county of chalk hills divided by broad
valleys and, in particular, by the valleys of the Stour
and the Frome. William Barnes is the poet of the
valleys, the elm and not the beech being his
favourite tree. In the first year of last century
he was born in Blackmoor Vale, which is watered
by a tributary of the Stour : at his death, only
fourteen years from the century's end, he was
rector of Came, which is in the valley of the Frome.
The son of a Dorset farmer, and for most of his life
a schoolmaster or clergyman within the county, the
Dorset dialect was his mother tongue, his " only true
speech." He wrote of Dorset, and for Dorset, and
strangers, perhaps natives also, might say that the
man was Dorset. His poems are full of the names
and the aspects of its towns and villages, its rivers
and brooks, and the hills that lie around its great

central height of Bulbarrow, which is mid-way between the homes of his childhood and old age.

In his " Praise o' Dorset " the poet is very modest, with a kind of humorous modesty, about the county. Though we may be homely, is the beginning, we are not ashamed to own our place ; we have some women " not uncomely," and so on. Homeliness, in fact, is characteristic of Barnes and of his Dorset. He became in some ways a learned man, but when he wrote in his mother tongue and from the heart, he was the Dorset farmer's son and nothing else. From the humble homeliness of his work he might have been a labourer, and he did more or less deliberately make himself the mouthpiece of the Dorset carters, cowmen, mowers, and harvesters. These songs, narratives, and dialogues bring forward the men at their labours, walking with their club flags to church, singing the songs of Christmas or Harvest Home. Here they court, wed, grow old together, build a new house, or return with money saved to their " poor forefathers' plot o' land." He celebrates the horses, Smiler, Violet, Whitefoot, Jack, and " the great old wagon uncle had." Separate poems are given to notable trees—" the great oak tree that's in the dell," the cottage lilac tree, the solitary may tree by the pond, an aspen by the river at Pentridge,

the great elm in the little home-field and its fall.
" Trees be Company " is the title of one of his
poems.

Many of his best passages are about old houses,
with hearths " hallowed by times o' zitten round,"
and fires that made the heart gay in storm or
winter, and some of them, like " the great old house
of mossy stone," with memories of stately ladies
that once did use

" To walk wi' hoops an' high-heel shoes "

along its terraces. It makes me think of a man
whose ancestors, at any rate, had often been cold,
homeless, and tired, when I see how often he speaks
of the hearth, the fire, the shelter of house walls,
at evening, in hard weather, or in old age. Again
and again ·he shows us the men forgetting their
work for a little while, as they sit among children
or friends, watching the flames in the window glass,
or listening to the wind and rain. Give me, he
says in one poem, even though I were the squire,
" the settle and the great wood fire." In another,
he feels that he can endure all if only evening
bring peace at home. A man with work, a family,
and a store of wood for the winter, has everything : the evening meal and the wife smiling
make bliss.

Barnes felt the pathos of the labourer's rest, and one of his finest poems depicts a cottage under a swaying poplar, with the moonlight on its door,—

> " An' hands, a-tired by day, wer still,
>   Wi' moonlight on the door."

He uses the same effect a second time, adding the reflection that the children now sleeping in the moonlit house will rise again to fun, and their widowed mother to sorrow. These people are pathetic because in their " little worold " they want and have so little,—

> " Drough longsome years a-wanderen,
>   Drough lwonesome rest a-ponderen."

Anything may eclipse, though nought can extinguish, their little joy ; yet they seem made rather for sorrow than joy. They have longings, but hardly passions. They want to rest after all, not to become discontented ghosts like " the weeping lady." They are prepared for the worst in this life, but the worst is tempered. The dead, for example, are safe from all weathers, better off than the bereaved who grieve for them " with lonesome love." The dead even seem beautiful in memory. There is a " glory round the old folk dead," the old uncle and aunt who used to walk arm in arm on Sunday

evenings about the farm, the grandmother who
wore " a gown with great flowers like hollyhocks,"
and told tales of ancient times, the old kindly squire
who so enjoyed life,—

> " But now I hope his kindly feäce
>   Is gone to vind a better pleäce."

Many poems are given to another and not very
different kind of memories, those of childhood,
and the essence of them, with a hundred pretty
variations, is,—

> " How smoothly then did run my happy days,
>   When things to charm my mind and sight were nigh."

Most are memories of the open air, of " lonesome
woodlands, sunny woodlands," the river and the
harvest fields, to the accompaniment of the songs
of birds and milkmaids. The children are always
laughing, playing, dancing in their " tiny shoes,"
but their heavy elders and the home under the elm
or in the " lonesome " grove of oak remind us, if
not them, of age and death.

The love-poems further illustrate Barnes's Dorset
homeliness and humbleness. Young maidens delight
him much as children do ; yet even while he is
praising the Blackmoor maidens he says,—

"Why, if a man would wive
  An' thrive, 'ithout a dow'r,
Then let en look en out a wife
  In Blackmwore by the Stour."

The girls all have something wifely about them. The wooer never forgets that the sweetheart may be the wife; he wishes her less care than her mother had, and looks forward to old age in her company. He is not a wild wooer. He is content to sit in a gathering and hear his Jane "put in a good word now and then," and have a smile and a blush from her at the door on parting: having carried her pail he is satisfied to know that she would have bowed when she took it back had it not been too heavy. He wants a maid who is "good and true," "good and fair," and healthy, and to have always beside him the "welcome face and homely name." Once he may have been ruffled by a mere beauty in a scarlet cloak, but probably he soon sets his heart on one who may bring him happiness with children, contentment with age, and perhaps help him to a little fortune in the thatched cottage "below the elems by the bridge." The lovers, like the poet himself, go with heads a little bowed, as if in readiness for blows. It is in contrast with these rather stiff, darkened men and women, who have winter and poverty on their horizon, that the children in Barnes's poetry are so blithe, his Spring days so buoyant, and his flowers and birds among the brightest and freshest in any of the poets.

But there is a greater than Duck or Barnes still among us, a wide-ranging poet, who is always a countryman of a somewhat lonely heart, Mr. Thomas Hardy. For I do notice something in his poetry which I hope I may with respect call rustic, and, what is much the same thing, old-fashioned. It enables him to mingle elements unexpectedly, so that, thinking of 1967 in the year 1867, he spoke not only of the new century having " new minds, new modes, new fools, new wise," but concluded,—

> "For I would only ask thereof
> That thy worm should be my worm, Love "—

which is as antique as Donne's Flea that wedded the lovers by combining blood from both of them within its body. The same rusticity manifests itself elsewhere as Elizabethanism, and the poet is something of a " liberal shepherd " in his willingness to give things their grosser names or to hint at them. He has a real taste for such comparisons as that made by a French officer looking at the English fleet at Trafalgar,—

> " Their overcrowded sails
> Bulge like blown bladders in a tripeman's shop
> The market-morning after slaughter-day."

Then, how his illustrations to his own poems—such as the pair of spectacles lying right across the landscape, following " In a Eweleaze near Weatherbury "—remind us of a seventeenth-century book of emblems !

Sometimes his excuse is that he is impersonating a man of an earlier age, as in the Sergeant's song,—

> " When Husbands with their Wives agree,
> And Maids won't wed from modesty,
> Then little Boney he'll pounce down,
> And march his men on London town.
>   Rollicum-rorum, tol-lol-lorum,
>   Rollicum-rorum, tol-lol-lay."

He has written songs and narratives which prove his descent from some ancient ballad-maker, perhaps the one who wrote " A pleasant ballad of the merry miller's wooing of the baker's daughter of Manchester," or " A new ballade, showing the cruel robberies and lewd life of Philip Collins, *alias* Osburne, commonly called Philip of the West, who was pressed to death at Newgate in London the third of December last past, 1597," to be sung to the tune of " Pagginton's round." Some of the lyric stanzas to which he fits a narrative originated probably in some such tune.

And how often is he delighted to represent a peasant's view, a peasant's contribution to the irony

of things, a capital instance being the Belgian who
killed Grouchy to save his farm, and so lost Napoleon
the battle of Waterloo.

With this rusticity, if that be the right name for
it, I cannot help connecting that most tyrannous
obsession of the blindness of Fate, the carelessness
of Nature, and the insignificance of Man, crawling
in multitudes like caterpillars, twitched by the
Immanent Will hither and thither. Over and over
again, from the earliest poems up to the " Dynasts,"
he amplifies those words which he puts into the
mouth of God,—

> " My labours, logicless,
>   You may explain ; not I :
> Sense-sealed I have wrought, without a guess
> That I evolved a Consciousness
> ` To ask for reasons why."

And, referring to the earth,—

> " It lost my interest from the first,
>   My aims therefor succeeding ill ;
> Haply it died of doing as it durst.
> Lord, it existeth still."

" Sportsman Time " and " those purblind Doom-
sters " are characteristic phrases. The many things
said by him of birth he sums up at the end of a
death-bed poem,—

" We see by littles now the deft achievement
    Whereby she has escaped the Wrongers all,
    In view of which our momentary bereavement
        Outshapes but small."

As gravely he descends to the ludicrous extreme of
making a country girl planting a pine-tree sing,—

        " It will sigh in the morning,
            Will sigh at noon,
        At the winter's warning,
            In wafts of June ;
        Grieving that never
            Kind Fate decreed
        It could not ever
            Remain a seed,
        And shun the welter
            Of things without,
        Unneeding shelter
            From storm and drought."

He puts into the mouths of field, flock, and tree—
because while he gazed at them at dawn they
looked like chastened children sitting in school
silent—the question,—

        " Has some Vast Imbecility,
            Mighty to build and blend,
            But impotent to tend,
        Framed us in jest, and left us now to hazardry ? "

Napoleon, in the " Dynasts," asks the question,
" Why am I here ? " and answers it,—

" By laws imposed on me inexorably.
History makes use of me to weave her web."

Twentieth century superstition can no farther go
than in that enormous poem, which is astonishing
in many ways, not least in being readable. I call
it superstition because truth, or a genuine attempt
at truth, has been turned apparently by an isolated
rustic imagination into an obsession so powerful
that only a very great talent could have rescued
anything uninjured from the weight of it. A
hundred years ago, Mr. Hardy would have seen
" real ghosts." To-day he has to invent them, and
call his Spirits of the Years and of the Pities,
Spirits Sinister and Ironic, Rumours and Record-
ing Angels, who have the best seats at the human
comedy, " contrivances of the fancy merely."

Even his use of irony verges on the superstitious.
Artistically, at least in the shorter poems, it may
be sound, and is certainly effective, as where the
old man laments on learning that his wife is to be in
the same wing of the workhouse, instead of setting
him " free of his forty years' chain." But the fre-
quent use and abuse of it change the reader's smile
into a laugh at the perversity.

Mr. Hardy must have discovered the blindness of
Fate, the indifference of Nature, and the irony of
Life, before he met them in books. They have

been brooded over in solitude, until they afflict him
as the wickedness of man afflicts a Puritan.   The
skull and crossbones, Death the scythed skeleton,
and the symbolic hour-glass have been as real to
him as to some of those carvers of tombstones in
country churchyards, or to the painter of that
window at St. Edmund's in Salisbury who represented " God the Father . . . in blue and red vests,
like a little old man, the head, feet, and hands
naked; in one place fixing a pair of compasses on
the sun and moon." If I were told that he had
spent his days in a woodland hermitage, though I
should not believe the story, I should suspect that
it was founded on fact.

But the woodland, and the country in general,
have given Mr. Hardy some of his principal con-
solations.   And one, at least, of these is almost
superstitious.   I mean the idea that " the longlegs,
the moth, and the dumbledore " know " earth-
secrets " that he knows not.   In the " Darkling
Thrush " it is to be found in another stage, the
bird's song in Winter impelling him to think that
" some blessed Hope " of which he was unaware
was known to it.   He compares town and country
much as Meredith does.   The country is paradise in
the comparison; for he speaks of the Holiday Fund
for City Children as temporarily " changing their

urban murk to paradise." Country life, paradise
or not, he handles with a combination of power
and exactness beyond that of any poet who could
be compared to him, and for country women I
should give the palm to his " Julie-Jane,"—

> " Sing ; how 'a would sing,
>   How 'a would raise the tune,
> When we rode in the wagon from harvesting
>   By the light of the moon. . . .
>   Bubbling and brightsome eyed,
>   But now—O never again !
> She chose her bearers before she died
>   From her fancy-men."

Such a woman has even made him merry like his
fiddling ancestor, in the song of " The Dark-eyed
Gentleman,"—

> " And he came and he tied up my garter for me."

And what with Nature and Beauty and Truth he is
really farther from surrender than might appear in
some poems. His " Let me enjoy "—

> " Let me enjoy the earth no less
>   Because the all-enacting Might
>   That fashioned forth its loveliness
>   Had other aims than my delight "—

is in the minor key, but by no means repudiates or
makes little of Joy, and is at least as likely as,

> " Lord, with what care hast thou begirt us round,"

to make a marching song.

VI.

ONCE in the night I awoke and heard the weir again, but the first sound in the morning was a thrush singing in a lilac next my window. For the main chorus of dawn was over. It was a still morning under a sky that was one low arch of cloud, a little whiter in places, but all gray. Big drops glistened on the undersides of horizontal rails. There had been a white frost, and, as they said, we seldom have many white frosts before it rains again. But not until I went out could I tell that it was softly and coldly raining. Everything more than two or three fields away was hidden.

Cycling is inferior to walking in this weather, because in cycling chiefly ample views are to be seen, and the mist conceals them. You travel too quickly to notice many small things; you see nothing save the troops of elms on the verge of invisibility. But walking I saw every small thing one by one; not only the handsome gateway chestnut just fully dressed, and the pale green larch plantation where another chiff-chaff was singing, and the tall elm tipped by a linnet pausing and musing a few notes, but every primrose and celandine and dandelion on the banks, every silvered green leaf of honey-suckle up in the hedge, every patch of brightest moss, every luminous drop on a thorn tip. The world seemed a small place : as I went between a row of elms and a row of beeches occupied by rooks, I had a feeling that the road, that the world itself, was private, all theirs ; and the state of the road under their nests confirmed me. I was going hither and thither to-day in the neighbourhood of my stopping place, instead of continuing my journey.

At a quarter-past nine it drizzled slightly more, but by ten the sky whitened, the grass gleamed. Over the broad field where the fowls and turkeys feed, and a retriever guards them, the keeper was walking slow and heavy, carrying a mattock, and after him two men, one in gaiters. While they were disappearing from sight in the corner where the field runs up into the wood, the chained retriever stood and whined piteously after them. I understood him very well. And somehow the men setting out thus for a day's work in the woods prophesied fine weather. Yet at half-past ten the

gray   n again to the horizon,
where   selves against it.

The   t at eleven, and shone
upon a   mustard and a man
loading   ceased to bend my
back and   ls violet, primrose,
anemone,   y in the blackthorn
hedges, and   sun have a chance with me.
I was trespassing, but, alas! no glory any longer
attaches to trespassing, because every one is so
civil unless you are a plain or ill-dressed woman,
or a child, or obviously a poet. So I came well-
warmed to Rudge, a hamlet collected about a
meeting of roads and scattered up a steep hill,
along one of these roads. The collection includes a
small inn called the "Half Moon," a plain Baptist
chapel, several stone cottages, several ruins, solid
but roofless, used solely to advertise sales, and a
signpost pointing to Berkley and Frome past the
ruined cottages, to Westbury and Bradley downhill from the inn, through the woods about the
river Biss, and uphill to Road and Beckington.
Southward I saw the single bare hump of Cley Hill
five miles away, near Warminster: northward, the
broad wooded vale rising up to hills on the horizon.
I went uphill, between two bright trickles of water.
The steep roadside bank, strengthened by a stone

wall, was well-grown with pennywort and cranes-
bill, overhung by goose grass and ivy, and bathed
at its foot by grass and nettles. The wall in one
place is hollowed out into a cavernous, dark dip-
well or water-cupboard. The rest of the village is
built upon the banks. First comes a Wesleyan
chapel, a neat, cold, demure little barn of the
early nineteenth century, having a cypress on
either side of its front door, and a few gravestones
round about. One of these caught my eye with the
verse—

> " And am I born to die,
>   To lay this body down,
>   And must my trembling spirit fly
>   Into a world unknown ? "—

and the name of Mary Willcox, who died in 1901 at
the age of eighty-eight. A cottage or two stand
not quite opposite, behind gardens of wallflowers,
mezereon, periwinkle, and tall copper-coloured
peony shoots, and a wall smothered in snow-on-the-
mountains or alyssum. On the same side, beyond,
a dark farm-house and its outbuildings project and
cause the road and water to twist. The bank on
that side, the left, covered with celandines and
topped with elms, now carries a footpath of broad
flagstones a yard or two above the road. Where
this footpath ends, the road, still ascending, forks,

and at once rejoins itself, thus making a small triangular island, occupied by a ruinous, ivy-mantled cottage and a cultivated vegetable garden. At the lower side a newish villa with a piano faces past the ruin uphill. At the upper side, facing past the ruin and the villa downhill, is a high-walled stone house of several gables, small enough, but possessing dignity and even a certain faint grimness : it is backed on the roadside by farm buildings. I saw and heard nobody from the " Half Moon " to this house, except a chicken. Here I turned off from the road along a lane which ended a mile away at a cottage and a farm-house, and in one of the ploughed fields I came upon a plain stone tower, consisting of two storeys, round-arched, roofless, in the company of a tall lime tree. It looks over the low land towards the White Horse at Westbury. Once, they told me, the upper storey held a water tank ; but as the map shows an ancient beacon at about this spot, I thought of it as a beacon rather than as a water tower.

I returned and went some way along the road to Beckington. A few people were walking in towards Rudge, children were picking primroses from both sides of the hedges, watched silently and steadfastly by a baby in a perambulator, not less happy in the sun than they. For the sun shone radiant and warm out of a whitewashed sky on the red ploughlands and wet daisy meadows by Seymour's Court Farm, on the teams pulling chain harrows and pewits plunging round them, and on the flag waving over Road Church as if for some natural festival. I found my first thrush's egg of the year along this road, in which I was fortunate; for the bank below the nest had been trodden into steps by boys who had examined it before me.

I went downhill again through Rudge and took the road for North Bradley, keeping above the left bank of the river Biss and commanding the White Horse on the pale wall of the Plain beyond it. This took me past Cutteridge, a modest farm, all that remains of a great house, whose long avenues of limes, crooked and often as dense as a magpie's nest, still radiate from it on three sides. This is a country of noble elms, spreading like oaks, above celandine banks.

Turning to the right down a steep-sided lane after passing Cutteridge I reached the flat, rushy, and willowy green valley of the Biss. The road forded the brook and brought me up into the sloping court-yard of Brook House Farm. On the right was a high wall and a pile of rough cordwood against it; on the left a buttressed, ecclesiastical-looking building with tiers of windows and three doorways, some four or five centuries old; and before me, at the

top of the yard, between the upper end of the high
wall and the ecclesiastical-looking building, was the
back of the farm-house, its brass pans gleaming.
This is the remnant of Brook House.   What is now
a cowshed below, a cheese room above, has been
the chapel of Brook House, formerly the seat of
Paveleys, Joneses, and Cheneys.   The brook below
was once called Baron's brook on account of the
barony conferred on the owner :   the family of
Willoughby de Broke are said to have taken their
name from it.   The cows made an excellent con-
gregation, free from all the disadvantages of
believing or wanting to believe in the immortality
of the soul, in the lower half of the old chapel ; the
upper floor and its shelves of Cheddar cheeses of all
sizes could not offend the most jealous deity or his
most jealous worshippers.   The high, intricate rafter-
work of the tiled roof was open, and the timber,
as pale as if newly scrubbed, was free from cob-
webs—in fact, chestnut wood is said to forbid cob-
webs.   Against the wall leaned long boards bearing
the round stains of bygone cheeses.   Every one
who could write had carved his name on the stone.
Instead of windows there were three doors in the
side away from the quadrangle, as if at one time
they had been entered either from a contiguous
building or by a staircase from beneath.   Evidently

both the upper and the lower chambers were formerly subdivided into cells of some kind.

The farm-house is presumably the remnant of the old manor house, cool and still, looking out away from the quadrangle over a garden containing a broad, rough-hewn stone disinterred hereby, and a green field corrugated in parallelograms betokening old walls or an encampment. The field next to this is spoken of as a churchyard, but there seems to be no record of skeletons found there. Half a mile off in different directions are Cutteridge, Hawkeridge, and Storridge, but nothing nearer in that narrow, gentle valley. . . .

The afternoon was as fine as Easter Monday could be, all that could be desired by chapel-goers for their Anniversary Tea. It was the very weather that Trowbridge people needed on Good Friday for a walk to Farleigh Castle, for beer or tea and watercress at the "Hungerford Arms." As I bicycled into Trowbridge at four o'clock the inhabitants were streaming out along the dry road westward.

I am not fond of crowds, but this holiday crowd caused no particular distaste. Away from their town and separated into small groups they had no cumulative effect. They were for the time being travellers as much as I was. In any case, a town like Trowbridge is used to strangers of all kinds passing through it : it would take a South Sea Islander in native costume to make it stare as a village does. The crowd that I dislike most is the crowd near Clapham Junction on a Saturday afternoon. Though born and bred a Clapham Junction man, I have become indifferently so. Perhaps I ought to call my feeling fear : alarm comes first, followed rapidly by dislike. It is a crowd of considerable size, consisting of women shopping, of young men and women promenading, mostly apart, though not blind to one another, and of men returning from offices. They take things fairly easily, even these last, and can look about. I shall not pretend to define the difference between them and a village or a provincial town crowd. It is less homely than a village, less compact and abounding in clear types than a town. It is a disintegrated crowd, rather suspicious and shy perhaps, where few know, or could guess much about, the others. When I find myself among them, I am more confused and uneasy than in any other crowd. I cannot settle down in it to notice the three or four or half a dozen types, as I should do at Swindon, or Swansea, or Coventry ; nor yet to please myself as with the general look of a village mob of forty or fifty, and a few of the most remarkable individuals. Here, at Clapham Junction, each one asks a separate question. In a quarter of an hour I am bewildered and dejected.

How different it is from a London crowd. In London everybody is a Londoner. Once in the Strand or Oxford Street I am as much at home as any one. If I were to walk up and down continuously for a week I should not be noticed any more than I am now. For all they know I am an Old Inhabitant. So is every one else from Cartmel or Tregaron. There are no lookers on : all are lookers on. I look hard at every one as at the pictures in a gallery, and no offence is taken. I can lose myself comfortably amongst them, and wake up again only when I find myself alone. Each day, except in the shops, an entirely new set of faces is seen, so far as memory tells me. A burly flower-girl, a white-haired youth, and a broken-down, long-haired actor or poet, are the only strangers in London I have seen more than once. Yet the combination is familiar. I am a Londoner, and I am at home. But I am not a Clapham Junction man any more than I am a Trowbridge man. Perhaps the reason of my discontent is that there are no Clapham Junction men, that all are strangers and aware of it, that they never truly make a mob like the factory men at New Swindon,

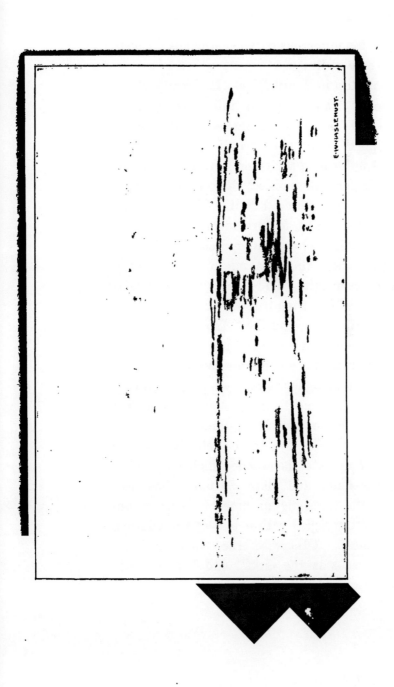

and yet are too numerous to be regarded as villagers like the people of Rudge.

I did not stop in Trowbridge. Its twenty chimneys were as tranquil as its tall spire, and its slaughter-house as silent as the adjacent church, where the poet Crabbe, once vicar, is commemorated by a tablet, informing the world that he rose by his abilities. In fact, the noisiest thing in Trowbridge was the rookery where I left it. Like nearly all towns—market towns, factory towns—Trowbridge is girdled by villas, chestnuts, and elms, and in the trees rooks build, thus making a ceremoniously rustic entrance or exit. While the rooks cawed overhead, the blackbirds sang below.

As far as Hilperton and the " Lion and Fiddle," houses and fields alternated along the road, but after that I entered a broad elmy country of young corn and new-ploughed land sweeping gradually away on my right up to grass slopes, and to the foot of dark Roundway Down and pale Beacon Hill, above Devizes. Far to the left the meadow land swelled up into the wooded high land above Lacock, Corsham, and Bath. Under elms near Semington the threshing-machine boomed; its unchanging note mingled with a hiss at the addition of each sheaf. Otherwise the earth was the rooks', heaven was the larks', and I rode easily

14

on along the good level road somewhere between the two.

Motion was extraordinarily easy that afternoon, and I had no doubts that I did well to bicycle instead of walking. It was as easy as riding in a cart, and more satisfying to a restless man. At the same time I was a great deal nearer to being a disembodied spirit than I can often be. I was not at all tired, so far as I knew. No people or thoughts embarrassed me. I fed through the senses directly, but very temperately, through the eyes chiefly, and was happier than is explicable or seems reasonable. This pleasure of my disembodied spirit (so to call it) was an inhuman and diffused one, such as may be attained by whatever dregs of this our life survive after death. In fact, had I to describe the adventure of this remnant of a man I should express it somewhat thus, with no need of help from Dante, Mr. A. C. Benson, or any other visitors to the afterworld. In a different mood I might have been encouraged to believe the experience a fore-taste of a sort of imprisonment in the viewless winds, or of a spiritual share in the task of keeping the cloudy winds "fresh for the opening of the morning's eye." Supposing I were persuaded to provide this afterworld with some of the usual furniture, I could borrow several visible things

from that ride through Semington, Melksham, and
Staverton. First and chief would be the Phœnix
"Swiss" Milk Factory where I crossed the Avon
at Staverton. It is an enormous stone cube, with
multitudinous windows all alike, and at the back
of it two tall chimneys. The Avon winding at its
foot is a beautiful, willowy river. On the opposite
side of the road and bridge the river bank rises up
steeply, clothed evenly with elms, and crowned by
Staverton's little church which the trees half
conceal. . . . This many-windowed naked mass,
surmounted by a stone phœnix, immediately over
the conspicuous information that it was burnt on
November 5, 1834, and rebuilt on April 28 of the next
year, is as big as a cathedral, and like a cathedral
in possessing a rookery in the riverside elms behind
it. With the small, shadowed church opposite, I
feel sure that it would need little transmutation to
fall into the geography of a land of shades. But the
most beautiful thing of all was the broad meadow
called Challimead on the west of Melksham, and
the towered church lying along the summit of the
gentle rise in which it ends. I bicycled along the
north-west side of it immediately after leaving
Melksham on the way to Holt. Elms of a hundred
years' growth lined the road, some upright, most
lying amid the wreckage of their branchwork far

out over the grass. Parallel with the road and much nearer to it than to the church the Avon serpentined along the meadow without disturbing the level three furlongs of its perfect green. The windows of the church flamed in the last sunbeams, the tombstones were clear white. For this meadow at least there should be a place in any Elysium. It would be a suitable model for the meadow of heavenly sheen where Æneas saw the blessed souls of Ilus and Assaracus and Dardanus and the bard Musæus, heroes and wise men, and the beautiful horses of the heroes, in that diviner air lighted by another sun and other stars than ours.

But our sun was fading over Challimead. The air grew cold as I went on, and the pewits cried as if it were winter. The rooks were now silent dots all over the elms of the Trowbridge rookery. A light mist was brushing over the fields, softening the brightness of Venus in the pale rosy west, and the scarlet flames that leapt suddenly from a thorn pile in a field. Probably there would be another frost to-night. . . . People were returning to the town in small and more scattered groups. At corners and crossways figures were standing talking, or bidding farewell. I rode on easily through the chill, friendly land. Clear hoofs hammering and men or girls talking in traps were but an added music to the quiet throughout the evening. I began to feel some confidence in the Spring.

I went out into the village at about half-past nine in the dark, quiet evening. A few stars penetrated the soft sky; a few lights shone on earth, from a distant farm seen through a gap in the cottages. Single and in groups, separated by gardens or bits of orchard, the cottages were vaguely discernible : here and there a yellow window square gave out a feeling of home, tranquillity, security. Nearly all were silent. Ordinary speech was not to be heard, but from one house came the sounds of an harmonium being played and a voice singing a hymn, both faintly. A dog barked far off. After an interval a gate fell-to lightly. Nobody was on the road.

The road was visible most dimly, and was like a pale mist at an uncertain distance. When I reached the green all was still and silent. The cottages on the opposite side of the road all lay back, and they were merely blacker stains on the darkness. The pollard willows fringing the green, which in the sunlight resemble mops, were now very much like a procession of men, strange primæval beings, pausing to meditate in the darkness.

The intervals between the cottages were longer here, and still longer; I ceased to notice them .

until I came to the last house, a small farm, where the dog growled, but in a subdued tone, as if only to condemn my footsteps on the deserted road.

Rows of elm trees on both sides of the road succeeded. I walked more slowly, and at a gateway stopped. While I leaned looking over it at nothing, there was a long silence that could be felt, so that a train whistling two miles away seemed as remote as the stars. The noise could not overleap the boundaries of that silence. And yet I presently moved away, back towards the village, with slow steps.

I was tasting the quiet and the safety without a thought. Night had no evil in it. Though a stranger, I believed that no one wished harm to me. The first man I saw, fitfully revealed by a swinging lantern as he crossed his garden, seemed to me to have the same feeling, to be utterly free of trouble or any care. A man slightly drunk deviated towards me, halted muttering, and deviated away again. I heard his gate shut, and he was absorbed.

The inn door, which was now open, was as the entrance to a bright cave in the middle of the darkness : the illumination had a kind of blessedness such as it might have had to a cow, not without foreignness ; and a half-seen man within it belonged to a world, blessed indeed, but far different from this one of mine, dark, soft, and tranquil. I felt

that I could walk on thus, sipping the evening
silence and solitude, endlessly. But at the house
where I was staying I stopped as usual. I entered,
blinked at the light, and by laughing at something,
said with the intention of being laughed at, I
swiftly again naturalized myself.

VII.

I AWOKE to hear ducklings squeaking, and a starling in the pine tree imitating the curlew and the owl hunting. Then I heard another chiff-chaff. Everything more than a quarter of a mile away was hidden by the mist of a motionless white frost, but the blackbird disregarded it. At a quarter to eight he was singing perfectly in an oak at the cross roads. The sun had melted the frost wherever it was not protected by hedges or fallen trees. Soon a breeze broke up and scattered and destroyed the mist, and I set out on a warm, cloudy morning that could do no wrong. As I was riding down the half-way hill between Trowbridge and Bradford, where the hedge has a number of thorns trimmed to an umbrella shape at intervals, they were ploughing with two horses, and the sun gleamed on the muscles of the horses and the polished slabs of the furrows. Jackdaws were flying and crying over Bradford-on-Avon.

I dismounted by the empty " Lamb " inn, with
a statue of a black-faced lamb over its porch, and
sat on the bridge. The Avon ran swift, but calm
and dull, down under the bridge and away westward. The town hill rises from off the water, covered as with scales with stone houses of countless
varieties of blackened gray and many gables, and
so steep that the roofs of one horizontal street are
only just higher than the doorsteps of the one above.
A brewery towers from the mass at the far side,
and, near the top, a factory with the words " For
Sale " printed on its roof in huge letters. And the
smoke of factories blew across the town. The
hilltop above the houses is crested with beeches
and rooks' nests against the blue. The narrow
space between the foot of the hill and the river
is occupied by private gardens, a church and its
churchyard yews and chestnuts, and by a tall
empty factory based on the river bank itself, with
a notice " To Let." Opposite this a small public
garden of grass and planes and chestnuts comes
to the water's edge, and next to that, a workshop
and a house or two, separated from the water by
rough willowy plots, an angle of flat grass and an
almond tree, and private gardens. Behind me the
river disappeared among houses and willows.

As I sat there, who should come up and stare at

the chapel on the bridge and its weather-vane of a
gilded perch, but the Other Man. Surprise sufficiently fortified whatever pleasure we felt to compel
us to join company ; for he also was going to Wells.

We took the Frome road as far as Winkfield,
where we turned off westward to Farleigh Hungerford. In half a mile we were in Somerset, descending by a steep bank of celandines under beeches
that rose up on our right towards the Frome. The
river lay clear ahead of us, and to our left. A
bushy hill, terraced horizontally, rose beyond it,
and Farleigh Hungerford Castle, an ivied front, a
hollow-eyed round tower, and a gateway, faced us
from the brow. From the bridge, and the ruined
cottages and mills collected round it, we walked
up to the castle, which is a show place. From here
the Other Man would have me turn aside to see
Tellisford. This is a hamlet scattered along half
a mile of by-road, from a church at the corner down
to the Frome. Once there was a ford, but now you
cross by a stone footbridge with white wooden
handrails. A ruined flock-mill and a ruined ancient
house stand next to it on one side ; on the other
the only house is a farm with a round tower em-
bodied in its front. Away from this farm a beautiful
meadow slopes between the river and the woods
above. This grass, which becomes level for a few

yards nearest the bank, was the best possible place, said the Other Man, for running in the sun after bathing at the weir—we could see its white wall of foam half a mile higher up the river, which was concealed by alders beyond. He said it was a great haunt of nightingales. And there was also a service tree; and, said he, in that tree sang a thrush all through May—it was the best May that ever was—and so well it sang, unlike any other thrush, that it made him think he would gladly live no longer than a thrush if he could do some one thing as right, as crisp and rich, as the song was. " I suppose you write books," said I. " I do," said he. " What sort of books do you write ? " " I wrote one all about this valley of the Frome. . . . But no one knows that it was the Frome I meant. You look surprised. Nevertheless, I got fifty pounds for it." " That is a lot of money for such a book ! " " So my publisher thought." " And you are lucky to get money for doing what you like." " What I like ! " he muttered, pushing his bicycle back uphill, past the goats by the ruin, and up the steps between walls that were lovely with humid moneywort, and saxifrage like filigree, and ivy-leaved toadflax. Apparently the effort loosened his tongue. He rambled on and on about himself, his past, his writing, his digestion ; his main point

being that he did not like writing. He had been
attempting the impossible task of reducing un-
digested notes about all sorts of details to a gram-
matical, continuous narrative. He abused notebooks violently. He said that they blinded him
to nearly everything that would not go into the
form of notes; or, at any rate, he could never
afterwards reproduce the great effects of Nature
and fill in the interstices merely—which was all
they were good for—from the notes. The notes—
often of things which he would otherwise have
forgotten—had to fill the whole canvas. Whereas,
if he had taken none, then only the important,
what he truly cared for, would have survived in
his memory, arranged not perhaps as they were in
Nature, but at least according to the tendencies of
his own spirit. "Good God!" said he. But luckily
we were by this time on the level. I mounted. He
followed.

Thanks, I suppose, to the Other Man's conversation, we took the wrong road, retracing our steps
to Farleigh instead of going straight on to Norton
St. Philip. However, it was a fine day. The sun
shone quietly; the new-cut hedges were green and
trim; neither did any of the prunings puncture our
tyres. Near the crossing from Wolverton to Freshford and Bath we sat down on a sheep trough and

ate lunch in a sloping field sprinkled with oak trees. The Other Man ate monkey-nuts for the benefit of his health, but pointed out that the monkey-nuts, like beef-steak, turned into himself. He informed me that he had been all over Salisbury on Saturday night and Bradford on Monday morning in a vain search for brown bread. But as the monkey-nuts had the merit of absorbing most of his attention he talked comparatively little. I was free, therefore, to look down over our field and over drab grass and misted copses southward to Cley Hill, a dim, broad landscape that seemed to be expecting to bring something forth.

We had not gone a mile from this stopping-place when the Other Man got off to look over the " George " at Norton St. Philip, another show place, known to its proprietor as " the oldest licensed house in England," and once for a night occupied by the Duke of Monmouth. It is a considerable, venerable house, timbered in front, with a room that was formerly a wool market extending over its whole length and breadth under the roof. In the rear of it crowded many pent-houses and outbuildings, equivalent to a hamlet, and once, no doubt, sufficient for all purposes connected with travel on foot or horseback. The Other Man was scared out of it in good time by a new arrival, a man of magnificent voice, who talked with authority, and without permission and without intermission, to any one whom neighbourhood made a listener. After a wish that the talker might become dumb, or he himself deaf, the Other Man escaped.

We glided down the street to a little tributary of a tributary too pleasantly to stop at the church below, though it had a grand tower with tiers of windows. The rise following brought us up to where a road crosses from Wellow, and at the crossing stands a small isolated inn called " Tuckers-grave." Who Tucker was, and whether it was a man or a woman buried at the crossing, I did not discover. The next village was Falkland, a mile farther on. It is built around a green, on one side of which a big elm overshadows a pair of stocks and a low, long stone for the patient to sit upon, and at the side a tall one like a rude sculptured constable. A number of other great stones were distributed about the village, including two smooth and rounded ones, like flat loaves, on a cottage wall. The children and youths of the village were in the road, the children whipping tops of a carrot shape, the youths of seventeen or so playing at marbles.

From this high land—for since rising up away from Norton St. Philip we had always been over four hundred feet up, midway between the valleys of the Frome on the left and the Midford brook on the right—we looked far on either side over valleys of mist. The hollow land on the right, which contained Radstock coalfield, many elm trees, and old overgrown mounds of coal refuse, was vague, and drowsed in the summer-like mist : the white smoke of the collieries drifted slowly in horizontal bands athwart the mist. The voices of lambs rose up, the songs of larks descended, out of the mist. Rooks cawed from field to field. Carts met us or passed us coming from Road, Freshford, Frome, and other places, to load up with coal from the store by the side of the road, which is joined to the distant colliery by a miniature railway, steep and straight. But what dominated the scene was a tall square tower on the road. Turner's Tower the map named it. Otherwise at a distance it might have been taken for an uncommon church tower or a huge chimney. The Other Man asked twenty questions about it of a carter whom we met as we came up to it ; and the carter, a round-eyed, round-nosed, round-voiced, genial man, answered them all. He said it had been built half a century ago by a gentleman farmer named Turner, as a rival to Lord Hylton's tower which we could see on our left at a wooded hilltop near Ammerdown

House. Originally it measured two hundred and thirty feet in height. Mr. Turner used to go up and down it, but it served no other purpose, and in course of time more than half fell down. The long hall at the bottom became a club-room, where miners used to drink more than other people thought good for them. Finally Lord Hylton bought it: the club ceased. About a hundred feet of the tower survives, pierced by a few pointed windows above and doors below, cheap and ecclesiastical in appearance. Attached to it is a block of cottages, and several others lie behind.

We crossed the Frome and Radstock road, and raced down a straight mile that is lined on the left by the high park walls of Ammerdown House, and overhung by beeches. At the bottom only an inferior road continued our line, and that dwindled to a footpath. For the descent to Kilmersdon by this direct route is too precipitous for a modern road. We had to turn, therefore, sharp to the left along the road from Writhlington to Mells and Frome, and then curved round out of it to the right, and so under the railway down to Kilmersdon. Before entering the village the road bent alongside a steep wooded slope littered with ash poles. The bottom of the deep hollow is occupied by a church, an inn distinguished by a coat-of-arms, and the motto, " *Tant que je puis*," and many stone cottages strung about a stream and a parallelogram of roads. The church tower has three tiers of windows in it, and a blue-faced clock, whose gilt hands pointed to half-past three. There is a venerable and amusing menagerie of round-headed and long-headed gargoyles, with which a man could spend a lifetime unbored. Inside as well as outside the church the Jolliffe family, now represented by Lord Hylton, predominates, amid the Easter scent of jonquil and daffodil. For example, much space is given to the following verses, in memory of Thomas Samuel Jolliffe, lord of the Hundreds of Kilmersdon and Wellow, a " high-minded and scrupulously honourable gentleman," " of Norman original," who died in 1824 at the age of seventy-eight,—

> " A graceful mien, an elegant address,
> Looks which at once each winning charm express,
> A life where worth by wisdom polished shines,
> Where wisdom's self again by love refines :—
> A wit that no licentious coarseness knows,
> The sense that unassuming candour shows,
> Reason by narrow principles unchecked,
> Slave to no party, bigot to no sect.
> Knowledge of various life, of learning too,
> Thence taste, thence truth, which will from taste ensue ;
> An humble though an elevated mind,
> A pride, its pleasure but to serve mankind :

15

If these esteem and admiration raise,
Give true delight and gain unflattering praise,
In one bright view the accomplished man we see,
These graces all were thine and thou wert he."

If human virtue, as it appears from these lines, lies buried at Kilmersdon, it has a pleasant resting-place—pleasant partly on account of the neighbourhood of one Robert Twyford, a former Treasurer of St. Davids, and lord of this manor, who died in 1776, aged sixty-one,—

" The sweetness of his temper made him happy in himself, and he employed his abilities, his fortune, and authority in rendering others so; and those many virtues which constituted his felicity in this life will, we trust, through the merits of Christ, make him completely happy to all eternity."

It would be easier to invent Thomas Samuel Jolliffe than Robert Twyford. I should like to meet them both; but in Jolliffe's case my chief motive would be curiosity to see how far his virtues were due to time, place, and the exigencies of rhyme. A dialogue between Jolliffe and the writer of his epitaph would be worth writing; equally so between the Treasurer of St. Davids and his—I can imagine the old man (I cannot imagine him a young man even in another world) beginning,—

" Sir, have you the felicity to know of a case where authority rendered any one happy save the exerciser of it ? I desire also, at your leisure, to know what you understand by the words, ' Completely happy to all eternity.' With as much impatience as is compatible with the sweetness of temper immortalized (to use a mortal phrase) by you at Kilmersdon, I await your answer. Will you drink tea ? But, alas ! I had forgotten that complete happiness in our present state has to be sustained without tea as well as without some of the other blessings of Pembrokeshire and Somerset. . . ."

" This is very sudden, Mr. Twyford. . . ."

What the Other Man most liked in the whole church was the small, round-headed window stained in memory of Sybil Veitch.

Out of Kilmersdon we walked uphill, looking back at the cottage groups in the hollow, the much-carved green slopes, and the high land we had traversed, all craggy-ridged in the mist. As steeply we descended to another streamlet, another hollow called Snail's Bottom, and the hamlet of Charlton and a rookery. Another climb of a mile, always in sight of a stout hilltop tower very dark against the sky, took us up to where the Wells road crosses a Roman road, the Fosse Way, now the road from Bath to Shepton Mallet. We chose the Fosse Way in order to see both Shepton and Wells. Thus we went through Stratton-on-the-Fosse, a high roadside village that provides teas, and includes a Roman Catholic college and a new church attached to it—that church whose tower we had been admiring so as it stood up against the sky. The flowering currant here was dressed in blossom.

A mile farther on we were seven hundred and twenty feet up, almost on a level with the ridge of the Mendips, now close before us. Running from that point down to Nettlebridge and its rivulet, and walking up away from them, was the best thing in the day. The gradient of the hillside was too much for a modern road. The Fosse Way, therefore, had been deserted and a new descent made, curving like an S; yet, even so, bold enough for a high speed to be attained before we got down to the "George" and the loose-clustered houses of Nettlebridge. The opposite ascent was also in an S. At the top of it we sat on a wall by the larches of Horridge Wood, and looked back and down. The valley was broad and destitute of trees. Gorse scrambled over its sides. Ducks fed across the turf at the bottom. Straight down the other side came the Fosse Way, denoted by its hedges, and round its crossing of the brook was gathered half of Nettlebridge. The rough, open valley, the running water, the brookside cluster of stone cottages, reminded me of Pembrokeshire. There is no church.

From that bleak and yet pleasant scene I turned with admiration to a farm-house on the other side of the road. It stood well above the road, and the stone wall enclosing its farm-yard followed the irregular crown of the steep slope. This plain stone house, darkened, I think, by a sycamore, and standing high, solitary, and gloomy, above Nettlebridge, seemed to me a house of houses. If I could draw, I would draw this and call it " A House." For it had all the spirit of a house, farm, and fortress in one, grim without bellicosity, tranquil, but not pampered.

Presently, at Oak Hill, we were well up on the main northern slope of the Mendips. The " Oak Hill " inn, a good inn, hangs out its name on a horizontal bar, ending in a gilded oak leaf and acorn. I had lunch there once of the best possible fat bacon and bread fried in the fat, for a shilling ; and for nothing, the company of a citizen of Wells, a hearty, strong-voiced man, who read the *Standard* over a beef-steak, a pint of cider, and a good deal of cheese, and at intervals instructed me on the

roads of the Mendips, the scenery, the celebrated
places, and also praised his city and praised the
stout of Oak Hill. Then he smacked his lips,
pressed his bowler tight down on his head, and
drove off towards Leigh upon Mendip. I was sorry
not to have arrived at a better hour this time.
The village is no more than the inn, the brewery,
and a few cottages, and a shop or two, in one of
which there was a pretty show of horse ornaments
of brass among the saddlery. I almost counted
these ornaments, crescents, stars, and bosses, as
flowers of Spring, so clearly did I recall their May-
day flashing in former years. It was darkening, or
at least saddening, as we rode out of Oak Hill
along the edge of a park which was notable for
much-twisted, dark sycamores on roots accumulated above-ground like pedestals. At the far side
gleamed the water, I imagine, of the brewery reser-
voir. We reached the main ridge road of the
Mendips soon after this, and crossed it at a point
about nine hundred feet high. Shepton is five
hundred feet lower, and but two miles distant; so
that we glided down somewhat like gods, having
for domain an expanse that ended in the mass of
Selwood Forest twelve miles to our left, level-
topped, huge, and dim, under a cloudy sky. Un-
prepared as I was, I expected to meet my end in

the steep conclusion of this descent, which was through narrow streets; and my brakes were bad. On the other hand, nothing troubled the god-likeness of my companion. In the rush at twenty-five miles an hour he sang, as if it had been a hymn of the new Paganism, a ribald song beginning,—

"As I was going to Salisbury upon a Summer's day."

When he had done he shouted across at me, " I would rather have written that song than take Quebec."

The Other Man would not stay in Shepton Mallet. He was very angry with Shepton. He called it a godless place, and I laughed, supposing he lamented the lack of Apollo or Dionysus or Aphrodite; but he justified the word by relating his first visit to the church. The bell was ringing. It was five minutes to eleven on a Wednesday, a day of north-east wind, in February. With him entered a clergyman, and except for the old bell-ringer, the church was empty. When the bells ceased at eleven it was still empty. The clergyman and the bell-ringer mumbled together, the old man saying, " You see, nobody has come." No service was held; the Other Man and the bell-ringer were unworthy. The clergyman struggled up the road against the north-east wind. " And

look there," exclaimed the Other Man, as we
turned out of the long, narrow street of shops into
Church Lane, mediæval-looking and narrower, " look
there," he exclaimed, pointing to the remains of a
blue election poster on a wall, where these words
survived,—

" Foreigners tax us ; let us tax them."

" Why," said he, " it is not even in the Bible,"
and with this he mountèd and rode on toward
Wells. The church tower was framed by the end
walls of Church Lane, a handsome, tall tower with
a pointed cap to it, and a worn statue of the Virgin
and two other figures over the door. Immediately
inside the door are tablets to seventeenth-century
and eighteenth-century Barnards and Strodes of
Down Hill, one bearing the inscription,—

" Urna tenet cineres
Animam deus."

The truth of it sounded like a copper gong in
that twilight silence. I went on among the ashes.
Two window ledges, one looking east, one west,
form couches for stone effigies. That in the eastward ledge, with his hand across the shield on his
breast, looked as if happily sleeping ; the other
had lost an arm, and was not happy. I re-entered
the main street by a side street broad enough for

a market-place. Here are some of the inns, and at the edge of the pavement a row of fixed wooden shambles. The market cross stands at the turn. It is a stone canopy, supported by six pillars in a circle, and one central pillar surrounded by two stone steps or seats, and the south side wears a dial, dated 1841. To know the yards of the " Red Lion," " George," and " Bunch of Grapes," and all the lanes and high-walled passages between Shepton and the prison, would be a task (for the first ten years of life) very cheerful to look back upon, and it would be difficult to invent anything more amusing and ingenious, as it would be impossible to invent anything prettier than the ivy, the ivy-leaved toadflax, and that kidney-leafed cressy white flower, growing on the walls of the passages. There are no public lights in Shepton, so that away from the shop lamps all now was dark in the side streets and edges of the town. The stone prison and all its apertures, like a great wasps' nest, was a punishment to look at in the darkness. But night added grandeur to the many round arches of the viaduct on which the railway strides across the valley. At this, a sort of boundary to Shepton upon the east, I turned back, and ended the day at a temperance hotel. Its plain and not old-looking exterior, ordinary bar and public room, suggested nothing of the ancientness within. I found a good fire and peace in the company of a man who studied Bradshaw. With the aid of maps I travelled my road again, dwelling chiefly on Tellisford, its white bridge over the Frome, the ruined mill and cottage, the round tower of Vaggs Hill Farm, and the distinct green valley which enclosed them, and after this, the Nettlebridge valley and the dark house above it.

VIII.

DAY opened cold, dull, and windy in Shepton Mallet. After paying the usual bill of about four shillings for supper, bed, and breakfast, I tried to get into the churchyard again ; but it was locked, and I set out for Wells. The road led me past the principal edifice in Shepton on the west side, as the prison is on the east—the Anglo-Bavarian Brewery, which is also the highest in position. It is a plain stone heap and a tubular chimney-stack of brick. A lover of size or of beer at any price might love it, but no one else. I rode from it in whirls of dust down to Bowlish and into the valley of the Sheppey. To within a mile of Wells I was to have this little river always with me and several times under me. Telegraph posts also accompanied the road. It was a delightful exit ; the brewery was behind me, a rookery before me in the beech trees of the outskirts. On both hands grassy banks rose up steeply. The left one, when the

rookery was passed, was topped with single thorn
trees, and pigs and chickens did their duty and
their pleasure among the pollard ashes below.   Most
of the cottages of Bowlish are on the other side,
their gardens reaching down in front of them to
the stream, their straggling orchards of crooked
apple trees behind within walls of ivy-covered
stone.   Where Bowlish becomes Darshill, the cottages are concentrated round a big square silk-mill
and its mill pond beside the road.   Up in the high
windows could be seen the backs or faces of girls
at work.   All this is on the right, at the foot of
the slope.   The left bank being steeper, is either
clothed in a wood of ivied oaks, or its ridgy turf
and scattering of elms and ash trees are seldom
interrupted by houses.   A sewage farm and a farm-
house ruined by it take up part of the lower slope
for some way past the silk-mill : a wood of oak and
pine invades them irregularly from above.   Then
on both hands the valley does without houses.   The
left side is a low, steep thicket rising from the
stream, which spreads out here into a sedgy pool
before a weir, and was at this moment bordered
by sheaves of silver-catkined sallow, fresh-cut.
But the right side became high and precipitous,
mostly bare at first, then hanging before me a rocky
barrier thinly populated by oaks.   This compelled

the road to twist round it in a shadowy trough. In fact, so much has the road to twist that a traveller coming from the other direction would prepare himself for scaling the barrier, not dreaming that he could slink in comfort round that wild obstacle.

Out of this crooked coomb I emerged into dust whirls and sunshine. The village of Crosscombe was but a little way ahead, a long village of old stone cottages and slightly larger houses, and two mills pounding away. The river running among stones sounds all through it. At the bridge, where it foams over the five steps of a weir, a drinking fountain is somewhat complicated by the inscription : "If thou knewest the gift of God, thou wouldest have asked of Him, and He would have given thee living water." At the " Rose and Crown," outside which is a cross, or rather a knobbed pillar surmounting some worn steps, I branched up a steep lane to St. Mary's Church. It has a spire instead of a tower, and an image of the Virgin at the base of it. Its broad-tailed weather-cock flashed so in the sun as to be all but invisible. The grass was at its greenest, the daisies at their whitest, in the churchyard, under the black cypress wedges, where lies something or other of many a Chedzoy, Perry, Hare, Hodges, and Pike. The upper side is bounded by a good ancient wall, cloaked in ivy and tufted with yellow wallflower. Another chiffchaff was singing here. While I was inside the building, a girl hung about, rattling the keys expectantly (but no more persuasively than the Titanic roadsters told their tale at Erlestoke), while I walked among the dark pews and choir stalls of carven oak, and looked at the tablets of the Hares and Pippets, great clothiers of this country, and the brass of Mr. William Bisse, and his nine daughters and nine sons, and Mrs. Bisse, in the costume of 1625. The church has a substantial business flavour belonging to the days when it was so little known as to be beyond dispute that blessed are the rich, for they do inherit this world and probably the next. A few yards higher up the slope from the church is a Baptist chapel and a cottage in one, evidently adapted with small skill or expense from a church building older than the sect. Nothing divided the vegetable garden of the cottage from the graveyard of the chapel, and it looked as if the people of Crosscombe were ill content to raise merely violets from the ashes of their friends.

The road climbed away from Crosscombe up the left wall of the valley, which is given a mountainous expression by the naked rock protruding both at the ridge and on the slope of Dulcote Hill. The

river runs parallel on the right beneath, and along
its farther bank the church and cottages of Dinder
in a string; and the sole noise arising from Dinder
was that of rooks. At a turning overshadowed by
trees, at Dulcote, a path travels straight through
green meadows to Wells, and to the three towers
of the cathedral at the foot of a horizontal terrace-
like spur of oak, pine, and beech, that juts out from
the main line of Mendip leftwards or southwards.
The river, which follows that main line up to this
spot, now quits it, and follows the receding left wall
of its valley, and consequently my road had its
company no longer. My way lay upward and over
the spur. The white footpath was to be seen going
comfortably below on the left through parklike
meadows, and beyond it, the pudding-shaped Hay
Hill and Ben Knowle Hill, and the misty dome of
Glastonbury Tor farther off.

By ten o'clock I was in the cathedral, and saw
the painted dwarf up on the wall kick the bell ten
times with his heel, and the knights race round
and round opposite ways, clashing together ten
times, while their attendant squires rode in silence;
and I heard the remote, monotonous priest's voice
in the *Benedicite*, and the deep and the high re-
sponses of men and boys. Up there in the tran-
septs and choir chapels are many rich tombs, and

recumbent figures overarched by stone fretwork;
but the first and lasting impression is of the clean
spaciousness of the aisles and nave, clear of all
tombs and tablets.

But clear and clean as was the cathedral, the
outer air was clearer and cleaner. The oblong
green, walled in on three sides by homely houses,
and by the rich towered west front on the fourth,
echoed gently with the typical cathedral music,
that of the mowing-machine, destroying grass and
daisies innumerable, with a tone which the sun
made like a grasshopper's, not out of harmony
with the song of a chaffinch asseverating whatever
it is he asseverates from one of the bordering lime
trees. The market-place, too, was warm; the
yellowish and grayish and bluish walls, the windows
of all shapes and all sizes, and the water of the
central fountain, answered the sun.

Two gateways lead out of one side of the market-
place to the cathedral and the palace grounds.
Taking the right-hand one, I came to the palace,
and the moat that flows along one side, between
a high wall climbed by fruit trees and ivy, and a
walk lined with old pollard elms. Rooks inhabited
the elm tops, and swans the water. Rooks are
essential to a cathedral anywhere, but Wells is
perfected by swans. On the warm palace roof

behind the wall—a roof smouldering mellow in the
sun—pigeons lay still ecclesiastically. ˉSometimes
one cooed sleepily, as if to seal it canonical that
silence is better; the rooks cawed; the water
foamed down into the moat at one end between
bowery walls. Away from the cathedral on that
side to the foot of the Mendips expanded low,
green country. I walked along the moat into the
Shepton road, and turning to the left, and passing
many discreet, decent, quiet houses such as are
produced by cathedrals, and to the left again, so
made a circuit of the cathedral and its high tufted
walls and holly trees, back to the market-place.

It was difficult to know what to do in all this
somewhat foreign tranquillity. I actually entered
an old furniture shop, and looked over a number of
second-hand books, *Spectators*, sermons that were
dead, theology that had never been alive, recent
novels preparing for their last sleep, books about
Wells, " Clarissa Harlowe," Mr. Le Gallienne's
" English Poems," " The Marvels of the Polar
World," and hundreds of others. A cat slept in
the sun amongst them, curled superbly, as if she
had to see justice done to the soporific powers of the
cathedral city and the books that nobody wanted.
For the sake of appearances, I bought " The History
of Prince Lee Boo " for twopence. I thought to

16

read this book over my lunch, but there was better
provender. The restaurant was full of farmers,
district councillors and their relatives, and several
school children. The loudest voice, the longest
tongue, and the face best worth looking at, belonged to a girl. She was a tomboy of fifteen,
black-haired, pale, strong-featured, with bold
though not very bright eyes. Her companion was
a boy perhaps a little younger than herself, and
she was talking in a quick, decided manner.

" I like a girl that sticks to a chap," she began
suddenly.

The boy mumbled something. She looked sharply
at him, as if to make sure that he did exist, though
he had not the gift of speech ; then directed her
eyes out into the street. Having been silent for
half a minute, she stood up, pressing her face to
the window to see better, and exclaimed,—

" Look, look ! There's lovely hair."

The boy got up obediently.

" There's lovely hair," she repeated, indicating
some one passing ; " she isn't good-looking to it,
but it is lovely now. Look ! isn't it ? "

The boy, I think, agreed before sitting down.
What impressed him most was the girl's frank
enthusiasm. She remained standing and looking
out. But in a moment something else had pleased

her. She beckoned to the boy, still with her eyes on the street, and said,—

" There's a nice little boy." As she said this she tapped the glass and smiled animatedly. So in half a minute up came another boy of about the same age as the first, and took a seat at the next table, smiling but not speaking. Only when he had half eaten a cake did he begin to talk casually about what had been passing at school—how an unpopular master had been ragged, but dared not complain, though nobody did any work. The girl listened intently, but when he had done, merely asked,—

" Have you ever been caned ? "

" Lots of times," he answered.

" Have *you* ? " she asked the boy at her own table.

" Once," he laughed.

" Have you ? " she mused. " I haven't. My mother told them they were to cane me at one school, and they did try once, but I never went back again after." . . . On finishing ·her lunch, she got up and strode out of the room silently, without a farewell. She was shorter than I had guessed, but more unforgettable than Prince Lee Boo. I put the book away unopened. Even what passes for a good book is troublesome to read after a few

days out of doors, and the highest power of most
of them is to convey an invitation to sleep. And
yet I thought of one writer at Wells, and that was
Mr. W. H. Hudson, who has written of it more
than once. He says that it is the only city where
the green woodpecker is to be heard. It comes
into his new book, '" Adventures among Birds,"
because it was here that he first satisfied his wish
to be in a belfry during the bell-ringing and hear
" a symphony from the days of the giants, composed (when insane) by a giant Tschaikovsky to
be performed on ' instruments of unknown form '
and gigantic size." But the book is really all
about birds and his journeys in search of them,
chiefly in the southern half of England. It is one
of his best country books. It is, in fact, the best
book entirely about birds that is known to me.
The naturalist may hesitate to admit it, though
he knows that no such descriptions of birds' songs
and calls are to be found elsewhere, and he cannot
deny that no other pages reveal English birds in
a wild state so vividly, so happily, so beautifully.
Mr. Hudson is in no need of recommendation
among naturalists. This particular claim of his
is mentioned only in order to impress a class of
readers who might confuse him with the fancy
dramatic naturalists, and the other class who will

appreciate the substantial miracle of a naturalist
and an imaginative artist in one and in harmony.

Were men to disappear they might be recon-
structed from the Bible and the Russian novelists;
and, to put it briefly, Mr. Hudson so writes of birds
that if ever, in spite of his practical work, his
warnings and indignant scorn, they should cease
to exist, and should leave us to ourselves on a
benighted planet, we should have to learn from
him what birds were.

Many people, even "lovers of Nature," would be
inclined to look for small beer in a book with the
title of "Adventures among Birds." If they are
ignorant of Mr. Hudson's writings, they are not to
blame, since bird books are, as a rule, small beer.
Most writers condescend to birds or have not the
genius to keep them alive in print, whether or not
they have the eternal desire " to convey to others,"
as Mr. Hudson says, " some faint sense or sugges-
tion of the wonder and delight which may be found
in Nature." He does not condescend to birds,
" these loveliest of our fellow-beings," as he calls
them, "these which give greatest beauty and lustre
to the world." He travels " from county to county
viewing many towns and villages, conversing with
persons of all ages and conditions," and when these
persons are his theme he writes like a master, like

an old master perhaps, as everybody knows, who
has read his " Green Mansions," " The Purple
Land," and " South American Sketches." It
might, therefore, be taken for granted that such an
artist would not be likely to handle birds unless
he could do so with the same reality and vitality as
men.   And this is what he does.

His chief pleasure from his childhood on the
Pampas has been in wild birds; he has delighted
in their voices above all sounds.   " Relations," he
calls the birds, " with knowing, emotional, and
thinking brains like ours in their heads, and with
senses like ours, only brighter.   Their beauty and
grace so much beyond ours, and their faculty of
flight which enables them to return to us each
year from such remote, outlandish places, their
winged, swift souls in winged bodies, do not make
them uncanny, but only fairy-like."

Only the book itself can persuade the reader of
the extraordinary love and knowledge of birds which
have thus been nourished.   If I were to quote the
passage where he speaks of his old desire to pursue
wild birds over many lands, " to follow knowledge
like a sinking star, to be and to know much until
I became a name for always wandering with a
hungry heart; " or where he declares that the
golden oriole's clear whistle was more to him

" than the sight of towns, villages, castles, ruins, and cathedrals, and more than adventures among the people ; " or where he calls being " present, in a sense invisible "—with the aid of silence and binoculars—" in the midst of the domestic circle of beings of a different order, another world than ours," nearly every one would probably pronounce him an extravagant sentimentalist, a fanatic, or, worst of all, an exaggerator. He is none of these. When he writes of his first and only pet bird and its escapes, there is no pettiness or mere prettiness : it is not on the human scale, yet it is equal to a story of gods or men. He is an artist, with a singular power of sympathizing with wild life, especially that of birds. Their slender or full throated songs, the " great chorus of wild, ringing, jubilant cries," when " the giant crane that hath a trumpet sound " assembles, the South American crested screamers counting the hours " when at intervals during the night they all burst out singing like one bird, and the powerful ringing voices of the incalculable multitude produce an effect as of tens of thousands of great chiming bells, and the listener is shaken by the tempest of sound, and the earth itself appears to tremble beneath him ; " the colouring of birds, brilliant or delicate, their soaring or manœuvring or straight purposed flight, their games and battles, all their joyous, or fierce, passionate, and agitated cries and motions, delight him at least as much as music delights its most sensitive and experienced lovers. At sight of the pheasant he cannot help loving it, much as he hates the havoc of which it is the cause.

There is a very large variety in his enjoyment. It is exquisite and it is vigorous; it is tender and at times almost superhuman in grimness. It is a satisfaction of his senses, of his curious intelligence, and of his highest nature. The green eggs of the little bittern thrill him "like some shining supernatural thing or some heavenly melody." He is cheerful when his binoculars are bringing him close to birds " at their little games "—a kestrel being turned off by starlings, a heron alighting on another heron's back, a band of starlings detaching themselves from their flock to join some wild geese going at right angles to their course; for " the playful spirit is universal among them." The songs of blackbird, nightingale, thrush, and marsh warbler delight him, and yet at other times the loss of the soaring species, eagles and kites, oppresses him, and he speaks contemptuously of " miles on miles of wood, millions of ancient noble trees, a haunt of little dicky birds and tame pheasants." His vision of the Somerset of the lake-dwellers, of " the paradise

of birds in its reedy inland sea, its lake of Athelney,"
makes a feast for the eyes and ears. Moreover, he
is never a mere bird man, and the result of this
variety of interest and pleasure on the part of a
man of Mr. Hudson's imagination, culture, and
experience, is that while his birds are intensely
alive in many different ways, and always intensely
birdlike, presenting a loveliness beyond that of
idealized or supernaturalized women and children,
yet at the same time their humanity was never
before so apparent. The skylark is to him both
bird and spirit, and one proof of the intense reality
of his love is his ease in passing, as he does in
several places, out of this world into a mythic,
visionary, or very ancient world. This also is a proof
of the powers of his style. At first sight, at least
to the novice who is beginning to distinguish between styles without discriminating, Mr. Hudson's
is merely a rather exceptionally unstudied English,
perhaps a little old-fashioned. Nothing could be
farther from the truth. It is, in fact, a combination,
as curious as it is ripe and profound, of the eloquent
and the colloquial, now the one, now the other,
predominating in a variety of shades which make it
wonderfully expressive for purposes of narrative
and of every species of description—precise, humorous, rapturous, and sublime. And not the least

reason of its power is that it never paints a bird without showing the hand and the heart that paints it. It reveals the author in the presence of birds just as much as birds in the presence, visible or invisible, of the author. The series of his books is now a long one, not enough, certainly, yet a feast, and the last is among the three or four which we shall remember and re-read most often.

I left Wells by a road passing the South-Western Railway station, and admired the grass island parting the roads to the passengers' and the goods' entrances. The curved edge of the turf was as clean as that of the most select lawn; the grass looked as if it had never been trodden. I now rode close to Hay Hill on my right—a dull, isolated heave of earth, striped downwards by hedges so as to resemble a country umbrella and its ribs. Motor cars overtook me. At Coxley Pound I overtook a peat-seller's cart. The air was perfumed with something like willow-plait which I did not identify. The wind was light, but blew from behind me, and was strong enough to strip the dead ivy leaves from an ash tree, but not to stop the tortoiseshell butterfly sauntering against it.

For three miles I was in the flat green land of Queen's Sedgemoor, drained by straight sedgy watercourses, along which grow lines of elm, willow, or pine. Glastonbury Tor mounted up out of the flat before me, like a huge tumulus, almost bare, but tipped by St. Michael's tower. Soon the ground began to rise on my left, and the crooked apple orchards of Avalon came down to the roadside, their turf starred by innumerable daisies and gilt celandines. Winding round the base of the Tor, I rode into Glastonbury, and down its broad, straight hill past St. John the Baptist Church and the notoriously mediæval "Pilgrim's Inn," and many pastry cooks. Another peat cart was going down the street. The church stopped me because of its tower and the grass and daisies and half-dozen comfortable box tombs of its churchyard, irregularly placed and not quite upright. One of the tombs advertised in plain lettering the fact that John Down, the occupant, who died in 1829 at the age of eighty-three, had "for more than sixty years owned the abbey." He *owned* the abbey, nothing more ; at least his friends and relatives were content to introduce him to posterity as the man who "for more than sixty years owned the abbey." If the dead were permitted to own anything here below, doubtless he would own it still. Outside the railings two boys were doing the cleverest thing I saw on this journey. They were keeping a whip-top, and that a carrot-shaped one, spinning by

kicking it in turns. Which was an accomplish·
ment more worthy of being commemorated on a
tombstone than the fact that you owned Glastonbury Abbey. The interior of the church is made
equally broad at both ends by the lack of screen or
of any division of the chancel. It is notable also
for a marble monument in the south-west corner,
retaining the last of its pale blue and rose colouring. A high chest, carved with camels, forms the
resting-place for a marble man with a head like
Dante's, wearing a rosary over his long robes.

At first I thought I should not see more of the
abbey than can be seen from the road—the circular
abbot's kitchen with pointed cap, and the broken
ranges of majestic tall arches that guide the eye to
the shops and dwellings of Glastonbury. While
I was buying a postcard the woman of the shop
reminded me of Joseph of Arimathea's thorn, and
how it blossomed at Christmas. " Did you ever
see it blossoming at Christmas ? " I asked. " Once,"
she said, and she told me how the first winter she
spent in Glastonbury was a very mild one, and she
went out with her brothers for a walk on Christmas
day in the afternoon. She remembered that they
wore no coats. And they saw blossom on the holy
thorn. After all, I did go through the turnstile to
see the abbey. The high pointed arches were mag·

nificent, the turf under them perfect. The elms stood among the ruins like noble savages among Greeks. The orchards hard by made me wish that they were blossoming. But excavations had been going on ; clay was piled up and cracking in the sun, and there were tin sheds and scaffolding. I am not an archæologist, and I left it. As I was approaching the turnstile an old hawthorn within a few yards of it, against a south wall, drew my attention. For it was covered with young green leaves and with bright crimson berries almost as numerous. Going up to look more closely, I saw what was more wonderful—Blossom. Not one flower, nor one spray only, but several sprays. I had not up till now seen even blackthorn flowers, though towards the end of February I had heard of hawthorn flowering near Bradford. As this had not been picked, I conceitedly drew the conclusion that it had not been observed. Perhaps its conspicuousness had saved it. It was Lady Day. I had found the Spring in that bush of green, white, and crimson. So warm and bright was the sun, and so blue the sky, and so white the clouds, that not for a moment did the possibility of Winter returning cross my mind.

Pleasure at finding the May sent me up Wearyall Hill, instead of along the customary road straight

out of Glastonbury. The hill projects from the
earth like a ship a mile long, whose stern is buried
in the town, its prow uplifted westward towards
Bridgwater; and the road took me up as on a
slanting deck, until I saw Glastonbury entire below
me, all red-tiled except the ruins and the towers
of St. John and St. Benedict. At the western edge
the town's two red gasometers stood among blossoming plum trees, and beyond that spread the
flat land. The Quantocks, fifteen miles distant,
formed but a plain wall, wooded and flat-topped,
on the horizon northward.

Instead of continuing up the broad green deck
of Wearyall Hill, I went along the west flank of
it by road, descending through meadows and apple
trees to the flat land. I crossed the river Brue
immediately by Pomparles bridge, and in half a
mile was in the town of Street. It is a mostly new
conglomeration of houses dominated by the chimney and the squat tower of Clark's Boot Factory;
and since it is both flat and riverless, it sprawls
about with a dullness approaching the sordid. A
rough-barked elm tree, a hundred and fifty years
old, slung on a timber carriage outside the "Street
Inn," was the chief sign of Spring here after the
dust.

I was very glad to see the flat slowly swelling

up at last to the long ridge of the Polden Hills, which was soon to carry my road. Walton, the next village, is a winding hamlet of thatched cottages, pink, yellow, and stone-coloured, alternating with gardens, plums in blossom, the vicarage trees and shrubbery, and the green yard of a quaint apsidal farmhouse, once the parsonage. It has a flagged pavement on the right, trodden solely by a policeman. The road was in the power of a steam-roller and its merry men, but the fowls of the old parsonage presented the only immediate signs of life. The plum blossom and new green leaves in hedge and border were spotless at Walton, its wallflowers very sweet on the untroubled air.

Thus I came clear of Street and the flat land. Outside of Walton I was in a country consisting of ups and downs rather than undulations, a grass country mainly, with orchards and hedges, elms in the hedges, pigs and sheep in the orchards. After the flat it was blessed. Perhaps it was not beautiful. It had character, but without easily definable features, and it fell an easy victim to such an accident as the absurdly dull stucco " Albion " inn, which appeared to have been designed for Pevensey or Croydon. Nevertheless, a sloping orchard of bowed apple trees sweeping the grass with their long, arched branches, and the smell

of peat smoke, counterbalanced the " Albion." At
Ashcott, where a man is free to choose between
very good water from a fountain on the right and
the coloured drinks of the " Bell " opposite, I was
two hundred feet up. I went into the church—
a delightful place for a retired deity—and enjoyed
this inscription on an oval tablet of marble, behind
the pulpit, relating to the " remains " of Joseph
Toms, who died in 1807, at the age of sixteen,—

" This youth was an apprentice to a grocer in Bristol, and
as long as health permitted proved that inclination no less
than duty prompted the union of strict integrity with industry.
During his illness unto death he was calm, resigned, and full
of hope. His late master has erected this small tribute to
perpetuate the worth of so promising a character."

My road ran along the ridge of the Poldens, and,
after Ashcott, touched but a solitary house or two.
One set of villages lay to the south or left, just
above the levels of Sedgemoor, but below the hills.
Another set lay below to the north, each with its
attendant level—Shapwick Heath, Catcott Heath,
Edington Heath, Chilton Moor, Woolavington
Level—beyond. Shapwick I turned aside to visit.
The village is scattered along a parallelogram of
roads and cross lanes. An old manor house, low
and screened by cedars, stands apart. The church,
of clean, rough stone, with a central tower, is in a

cedared green space at a corner, having roads on
two sides, a farm and an apple orchard on the
others ; and trees have supplanted cottages on one
roadside. A flagged path leads among the tombstones to the church door. One of the inscriptions
that caught my eye was that in memory of Joe
Whitcombe, fifty years a groom and factotum in
the Strangways family at the manor house, who
died at the age of sixty-four in 1892. Along with
these facts are the lines,—

> "An orchard in bloom in the sunny spring
> To me is a wondrous lovely thing."

Very different from Old Joe's are the epitaphs inside
the church, the work largely, I believe, of a former
vicar, G. H. Templer, who built the big blank vicarage
with its square, high-walled fruit garden and double
range of stables, and planted cedars and cork
trees. The epitaph of Lieut.-Col. Isaac Easton of
the East India Company is a fair sample of this
practically imperishable prose,—

"Through all the gradations of military duty, his love of
Enterprise, his Valour, his Prudence, and Humanity, obtained
the admiration and affection of his fellow-soldiers with the
confidence and commendation of that government which knew
as well to distinguish as to reward real merit. In the more
familiar walks of private life, all who knew him were eager to
approve and to applaud the brilliant energy of his mind and

17

the polished affability of his manners. His heart glowed with
al lthe sensibility which forms the genuine source of real goodness and greatness, with gratitude to his benefactor, with
generosity to his friend, and liberality to mankind. The
sudden loss of so many virtues and so many amiable qualities,
who that enjoyed his confidence or shared his conviviality
can recall without a sigh or a tear ? With a constitution im-
paired by the severities of unremitted service and the rigours
of an oppressive climate, he returned, to the fond hope of enjoying on his native soil the well-earned recompense of his
honourable labours, when a premature death hurried him to
his grave in 1780, at the age of 45."

Templer's position in prose is the same as that
of Jolliffe's encomiast in verse at Kilmersdon. The
relation of his work to life at Shapwick in the
eighteenth century is about as close as that of the
" Arcadia " to Sidney's age. More telling are the
inscriptions of two men named Cator and Graham,
who were killed during a fight with a French
privateer in the Bay of Bengal in October 1800.
The Bulls and Strangways have big slabs ; the
Bulls adding the blue and crimson of their arms to
the chancel. Not less silent than the church was
the street leading down towards the manor house
and railway station, silent except for a transitory
twitter of goldfinches. The one shop had its blinds
drawn in honour of early closing day. It is a
peaceful neighbourhood, where every one brews his
own cider and burns the black or the inflammable

ruddy peat from the moor. A corner where there are a beautiful chestnut and some waste grass provides a camping ground for gypsies from Salisbury and elsewhere; and it seemed fitting that men and boys should spend their idle hours in the lane at marbles. It is famous, if at all, since the battle of Sedgemoor, for giving a home to F. R. Havergal and an occasional resting-place to Churton Collins.

Very still, silvery, and silent was the by-road by which I rode up through ploughland back again to the ridge. Lest I had missed anything, I turned away from my destination for a mile towards Ashcott. I was for most of the distance in Loxley Wood. Primroses, as far as I could see, clustered thick round the felled oaks, the fagot heaps, and the tufts of last year's growth on the stoles. A few stones on the right inside the wood are called Swayne's Jumps, and it is related that a prisoner of the name, whether in Monmouth's or Cromwell's time I forget, escaped by means of some tremendous jumps there, taken when he was pretending to show his captors how they ought to jump.

Even without the wood this road was beautiful. For it was bordered for some way on the left by a broad grass strip planted with oaks, and not common oaks, but trees all based on small moss-gilded pedestals of their own roots above the earth, their bark and branches silver, their main limbs velveted with moss and plumed with polypody ferns. Moreover, they have filled the few gaps with young trees. On the right, after coming to the end of Loxley Wood and before the signpost of Greinton, I saw a rough waste strip of uneven breadth, partly overgrown by bushes from the hedge and by pine trees. Here ran the rank of telegraph posts, and in the grass were remains of fires. A hundred yards later, and as far as the turning of Shapwick, the waste was quite a little rushy common fed by horses.

Turning once more westward and again piercing Loxley Wood, the wayside strip there consecrated to the oak avenue ceased, but that it had once been prolonged far along the road was plain, whether it had been swallowed up by wood or meadow, or hedged off and planted with larches or apple trees, or ploughed up, or usurped by cottage and garden. Shorn thus, the road travels four miles of a ridge as straight and sharp as the Hog's Back. It was delicious easy riding, with no company but that of a linnet muttering sweetly in the new-green larches, and a blackbird or two hurrying and spluttering under the hedge.

All the country on either hand was subject to my eyes. Before me the red disc of the sun was low,

its nether half obliterated by a long, misty cloud.
The levels on my right, and their dark, moss-like
corrugations, were misted over, not so densely that
a white river of train smoke could not be seen
flowing through it; and Brent Knoll far off towered
over it like an islet of crag, dark and distinct; nor
was the prostrate mass of Brean Down invisible
on the seaward side of Brent Knoll. Not a sound
emerged from that side beyond the bleat of a few
lambs. On the left was the misty country of
Athelney, and a solitary dark tower raised well above
the midst of the level. The most delicate scene of
all my journey was nearer. The Poldens have
on this side several foothills, and at the turning to
Righton's Grave one of these confronted me; I had
it in full view for a mile and could hardly look at
anything else. This was Ball Hill. It is a smooth
island lifted up out of an ever so faintly undulating
land of hedged meadows and sparse elm trees. It
rose very gradually, parallel to my road and about
half a mile from it, so as to make a long, nascent
curve, up to a comb of trees; and its flank was
divided downwards and lengthwise amongst rosy
ploughland and pale green corn in large hedgeless
squares and oblongs, beautifully contrasted in
size and colour. Next to Ball Hill is another one,
as distinct, but steeper and wooded, called Pendon

Hill. In the dip between the two lay the church tower and cottages of Stawell, and a dim orchard rose behind them with trees that were like smoke. Though the lines of these hills and their decorated slopes are definitely beautiful, during the dusk on that silver road in the first Spring innocence they were a miraculous birth, to match the Spring innocence and the tranquillity of the dusk as I slid quietly on that road of silver.

Then came two shams. The first was a towered residence close to the road, with Gothic features. The second, black against the sky, three miles ahead, was a tower and many ruinous arches on top of the wooded hill at Knowle. It is hard to show how not very experienced eyes begin to suspect a sham of this sort. But they did, and yet were able to dally a little with the kind of feeling which the real thing would have produced. For, when I saw the ruins most clearly, at the turn to Woolavington, Highbridge, and Burnham, twilight was half spent.

The road was descending. Bridgwater's tower, spire, and chimneys, and smoke mingling with trees, were visible down on the left, and past them the dim Quantocks fading down to the sea. I was soon at the level of the railway, and Bawdrip behind the embankment showed me a pretty jumble of roofs, chimneys, a church tower, and a green thorn tree over the rim. The high slope of Knowle and its rookery beeches—where the ruin is—hung upon the right very darkly over the small pale " Knowle Inn " and the white scattered blackthorn blossom and myself slipping by. The road went on to Puriton and Pawlett, and down it under the trees two lovers were walking slowly, but opposite Knowle I had to turn sharp to the left. Those green trees in the last of the twilight seemed exceptionally benign. After the turning I immediately crossed the deep-cut King's Sedgemoor drain—with a flowering orchard betwixt it and the road I had left—and in a few yards the single line of the Somerset and Dorset Joint Railway. Two miles of flat field and white-painted orchard, and I was in a street of flat, dull, brick cottages and foul smoke, but possessing an extraordinarily haughty white hart chained over an inn porch of that name. Then the river Parrett ; and a dark ship drawn up under the line of tall inns and stores with glimmering windows. I crossed the bridge and walked up Corn Hill between the shops to where the roads fork, one for Taunton, one for Minehead, to left and right of Robert Blake's statue and the pillared dome of the market. I took the Minehead road, the right-hand one, past the banks, the post office, the " Royal Clarence " hotel, and by half-past seven I was eating supper, listening to children outside in the still, dark street, laughing, chattering, teasing, disputing. I read a page or two of the " History of Prince Lee Boo," and fell asleep.

IX.

THE night at Bridgwater was still. I heard little after ten except the clear deep bells of St. Mary's telling the quarters. They woke me with the first light, and I was glad to be out of the hotel early because the three other guests (I think, commercial travellers) not only did not talk— which may have been a blessing—but took no notice of " Good evening " or " Good morning." It was a clean, new, and unfriendly place, that caused a sensation as of having slept in linoleum. The charge for supper, bed, and breakfast was the usual one, a few pence over four shillings.

I wandered about the western half of the town. This being built on a slight hill above the river, was older and better worth looking at than the flat eastern half, though it was lacking in trees, as may be guessed from the fact that some rooks had had to nest in horse-chestnut trees, which they avoid if possible. Castle Street is the pleasantest in the town, a wide, straight old street of three-storey brick houses, rising almost imperceptibly away from the quay. The houses, all private, have round-topped windows and are flat-fronted, except for two at the bottom which have bays. Across the upper end a big, sunlit, ivied house, taller than the others and of mellower brick, with a chestnut tree, projects somewhat, and on the pavement below it is a red pillar box.

The quay itself is good enough to recall Bideford. The river is straight for a distance, and separated from the quayside buildings only by the roadway. These buildings, ship-brokers' and contractors', port authority's and customs and excise offices, a steam sawmill, and the " Fountain," " Dolphin," and " King's Head," are plain enough, mostly with tall flat fronts with scant lettering and no decoration, all in a block, looking over at the low level of the Castle Field north-eastward, where cattle grazed in the neighbourhood of chimney-stacks and railway signals. The *Arthur* was waiting for a cargo. The *Emma* was unloading coal. But for the rest the quay was quiet, and a long greyhound lay stretched out across the roadway, every inch of him content in the warm sun.

The next best thing to the quay was the broad

sandstone Church of St. Mary and its tall spire,
standing on a daisied, cropped turf among thorns
and a few tombstones, and walled in on three
sides by houses, shops, and the " White Lion " and
" Golden Ball." The walls inside provide recesses
for many tombs. The most memorable tomb in the
church is that of an Irish soldier named Kingsmill.
He is a fine fellow, albeit of stone, leaning on his
elbow and looking at the world or nothing as if
satisfied with his position. He " sleeps well "—no
man, I should say, better. This and his features
reminded me of a man still living, a man of brawn
and spirit, a despiser of beastly foreigners, and a
good sleeper. I have seen him looking like old
Kingsmill, with this one difference—that when he
was in that stage of wakingness he had a cigarette
between his lips invariably. He awoke, smiling
at the goodness of sleep and of the world, and lay
back, whoever called him, to sleep again. Resur-
rected at length, or partly so, he would sigh,
but not in sorrow, and then swear, and turn over
to reach a cigarette from beside the bed. The
lighted cigarette regilded the world : he envied no
man, any more than Kingsmill does, and certainly
no woman. The cigarette, though enchanted, came
to an end, even so; and he did what Kingsmill
perhaps never did, took a cold bath, but in a

manner which Kingsmill would have admired. The
bath being filled to within an inch or two of
overflowing, he let himself slowly in until he was
completely under water, where he lay in a state
apparently of bliss lasting many seconds, for bene-
ficent providence had ordained that he should be
almost as much aquatic as he was earthly, worldly,
and territorial. Then out he came like Mars rising
from the foam. After drying himself for ten
minutes he lit another cigarette and rambled about
his room without artificial covering until he had
smoked it. Next he began dressing, an operation
not to be described in my style in less than two
volumes octavo, and worthy of something incom-
parably more godlike, for he was as a god and his
dressing was godlike. . . . After Kingsmill's effigy
the chief spectacle of St. Mary's is the unexpected,
big Italianate picture of Christ's descent from the
cross, which forms an altar-piece. The story is
that it was taken from a Spanish vessel—some add
that it was one of the Great Armada; that it
reached Bridgwater after a long seclusion at
Plymouth, and was claimed by Plymouth when
Bridgwater was seen to have it, but that Bridgwater kept it in a packing case for two years.

With the quay and the church ranks the statue of
Robert Blake, if only for the inscription,—

"Born in this town, 1598.
Died at sea, 1657."

I am told that there is also a passage quoted from
one Edmund Spencer, but I did not see it ; nor is
it so great an error as the inscription about Jefferies
in Salisbury Cathedral, and they have less time
in Bridgwater market-place than in Salisbury
Cathedral for literary accuracy.

It was half-past ten on a beautiful morning when
I rode out of the town by a very suburban suburb
of villas, elms, and a cemetery. My road carried
me at first along a low ridge, so that over the
stone walls I looked down, east and northward to
the vale of the Parrett ; a misty, not quite flat
expanse of green, alternating with reddish and
already crumbling ploughland, which was interrupted a mile away by the red walls, elms, and
orchard of Chilton Trinity, and farther off, by the
pale church tower of Cannington. Two horses
were drawing a scarifier across the furrows of a
field by the roadside. On my left or westward I
looked beyond a more broken country, with white
linen blowing on cottage garden bushes, to the dim
Quantocks still far off. The sun was hot, but the
wind blew from behind me, and the dust was not an
offence when a motor car was not passing me. A
chiff-chaff was singing at Wembdon. Larks crowded

their songs into a maze in every quarter. Overhead a single telegraph wire sizzled.

Three miles out of Bridgwater my road had dropped to the level, and proceeded over it to Cannington, but instead of sticking to it I turned at a smithy on my left into a by-road, which wound between low hedges of thorn and maple mounted either on ivied walls or on banks covered with celandines. It passed Bradley Green's few cottages, the " Malt Shovel " inn, an oak copse with a chiff-chaff in it, and here a robin on a wall, and there a linnet on a thorn tip, in a slightly up and down country of grass, ploughland, and orchard. In a mile the road twisted at right angles to cross the Cannington brook and rejoin the main road ; and at this angle, by a green bowered lane, was a stone house and chapel in one. This was Blackmoor Manor Farm, a group that no longer has anything stately or sacred save what it owes to its antiquity and continuous human occupation.

The main road, when I rejoined it, was rising once more between banks of gorse. So bright was the blossom of the gorse that its branches were shadowy and nearly invisible in the brightness. For the sun was now as warm as ever it need be for a man who can move himself from place to place. On both hands the undulating land was warm and misty, but particularly on the right. There, as I approached Swang Farm, at the third milestone from Nether Stowey, a hill, almost as graceful as Ball Hill near Stawell, rose parallel to the road, its long-curving ridge about a third of a mile away. Its smooth flank was apportioned by hedgerows and a few elms among bare ploughland and young corn above, and drabby grass with sheep on it below. Near by, on the other side, was another such hill, a nameless one above Halsey Cross Farm, which I first took notice of when it was cut in two perpendicularly by the signpost pointing to Spaxton. It was but a blunt, conical hillside of green corn, rosy ploughland, sheep-fed pasture, and a few elms in the partitions; and behind it the dim Quantocks. Between these two hills, at a spot where the road twists again at right angles, a brick summer-house perched on the walled roadside bank, at the very corner. Here, as I heard, a few generations ago, ladies from the house near by used to sit to watch for the coaches. I was now two hundred feet up in the foothills of the Quantocks. Three or four miles in front bulked the moorlands of the main ridge.

Nether Stowey begins with a church and a farm and farmyard in a group. Then follows a street of cottages without front gardens, dominated by a

smooth green " castle " rampart a third of a mile
away. The street ends in a " First and Last Inn "
on one side, and a cottage on the other, announced
as formerly Coleridge's by an inscription and a
stone wreath of dull reddish brown. Altogether
Nether Stowey offered no temptations to be compared with those of the road leading out of it.
Immediately outside the village it was walled by
deep banks, and on these grew arum, celandine, and
nettle, with bushes of new-leaved blackthorn and
spindle. Here I saw the first starry, white stitch-
worts or milkmaids. And henceforward I was
always walking steeply up or steeply down one of
the medley of lesser hills. Below on the right was
chiefly red ploughland ; above on the left wilder
and wilder heights of sheep-fed moorland. The
road was visible ahead, looping half way up the
slopes.

Honeysuckle ramped on the banks of the deep-
worn road in such profusion as I had never before
seen. The sky had clouded softly, and the sun-
warmed misty woods of the coombs, the noise of
slender waters threading them, the exuberant young
herbage, the pure flowers such as stitchwort and
the pink and " silver white " cuckoo flowers, but
above all the abounding honeysuckle, produced an
effect of wildness and richness, purity and softness,

so vivid that the association of Nether Stowey was hardly needed to summon up Coleridge. The mere imagination of what these banks would be like when the honeysuckle was in flower was enough to suggest the poet. I became fantastic, and said to myself that the honeysuckle was worthy to provide the honeydew for nourishing his genius; even that its magic might have touched that genius to life—which is absurd. And yet magic alone could have led Coleridge safely through the style of his age, the style of the author of Jolliffe's epitaph at Kilmersdon, the style of Stephen Duck and his benefactors, the style of his own boyish effusions, where he personified Misfortune, Love, Wisdom, Virtue, Fortune, and Content with the aid of capitals. He fell again when weary into lines like,—

"Thro' vales irriguous, and thro' green retreats;"

he rose and fell once more, until finally the conventions had either slipped away or been adopted or subdued. Perhaps it was not in vain, or so fatuous as it seems to us, that he personified, like any lady or gentleman of the day,—

"The hideous offspring of Disease,
Swoln Dropsy ignorant of Rest,
And Fever garb'd in scarlet vest;

18

> Consumption driving the quick hearse,
> And Gout that howls the frequent curse ;
> With Apoplex of heavy head
> That surely aims his dart of lead."

Whether we can follow him or not into intimacy with those " beings of higher class than man," Fire, Famine, Slaughter, Woes, and Young-eyed Joys, the more or less than fleshly creatures of his later poems may owe something to that early dressing up, as well as to the honeydew-fed raptures of Nether Stowey.

Some of the early poems reveal underneath the dismal tawdry vesture of contemporary diction the beginnings of what we now know as Coleridge. It is to be seen in the sonnet, " To the Autumnal Moon," written in 1788 when he was sixteen, which begins,—

> " Mild Splendour of the various-vested Night,
> Mother of wildly-working visions hail ; "

and then again more subtly in 1795, when he is looking for a Pantisocratic dell,—

> " Where Virtue calm with careless step may stray,
> And dancing to the moonlight roundelay,
> The Wizard Passions weave an holy spell " . . .

though it is impossible to say that the collocation of calm and careless, wizard and holy, would have

arrested us had Coleridge made no advance from
it, had he remained a minor poet. The combination
of mild and wild is a characteristic one, partly
instinctive, partly an intellectual desire, as he
shows by speaking of a " soft impassioned voice,
correctly wild." The two come quaintly together
in his image of,—

" Affection meek
(Her bosom bare, and wildly pale her cheek),"

and nobly in the picture of Joan of Arc,—

" Bold her mien,
And like a haughty huntress of the woods
She moved : yet sure she was a gentle maid."

Coleridge loved equally mildness and wildness, as
I saw them on the one hand in the warm red fields,
the gorse smouldering with bloom, the soft delicious greenery of the banks ; and on the other hand
in the stag's home, the dark, bleak ridges of heather
or pine, the deep-carved coombs. Mildness, meekness, gentleness, softness, made appeals both sen-
suous and spiritual to the poet's chaste and volup-
tuous affections and to something homely in him,
while his spirituality, responding to the wildness,
branched forth into metaphysics and natural magic.
Some time passed before the combining was complete. There was, for example, a tendency to

naiveté and plainness, to the uninspired accuracy
of " pinky-silver skin " (of a birch tree), and to
the matter of fact—

> " The Mariners gave it biscuit worms—"

which he cut out of " The Ancient Mariner." He
cut out of " This Lime-tree Bower my Prison," a
phrase informing us that he was kept prisoner by
a burn. At first he called " the grand old ballad of
Sir Patrick Spens " the " dear old ballad," and the
lines,—

> " Yon crescent Moon is fixed as if it grew
>   In its own cloudless, starless lake of blue "

were followed by—

> " A boat becalm'd, a lovely sky-canoe "

It was natural to him at first to address Wordsworth
as

> " O Friend ! O Teacher ! God's great gift to me ! "

and it became natural to him to cut out the last
phrase. Formerly Geraldine said to Christabel,
" I'm better now " ; and instead of lying entranced
she lay " in fits." The poem still includes the
phrase describing Christabel's eyes,—

> " Each about to have a tear ; "

while " Frost at Midnight " retains the allusion to

the " fluttering stranger " in the fire, the filmy blue
flame, as a note instructs us, " supposed to portend
the arrival of some absent friend." There is, too,
a whole class of homely poems, on receiving the
news of his child's birth, on being warned not to
bathe in the sea: "God be with thee, gladsome
Ocean," it begins.

The mildness, meekness, gentleness, beloved of
Coleridge's tender and effusive nature, appear with
such diverse company as in " Poverty's meek woe,"
" mild and manliest melancholy," and " mild moon-
mellow'd foliage," and repeated with variations four
times in one verse of the lines written at Shurton
Bars, near Bridgwater,—

> " I felt it prompt the tender Dream,
>   When slowly sank the Day's last gleam ;
>   You rous'd each gentler sense,
>   As sighing o'er the Blossom's bloom
>   Meek Evening wakes its soft perfume
>   With viewless influence."

Sometimes the mildness expands to conscious
luxury, as in the poem " Composed during Illness,
and in Absence," beginning,—

> " Dim Hour, that sleep'st on pillowing clouds afar,
>   O rise and yoke the Turtles to thy car !
>   Bend o'er the traces, blame each lingering Dove,
>   And give me to the bosom of my Love !

...e, caressing and carest,
...heart shall carol me to rest!
...tear-drop from her smiling eyes—
...woe, and medicine me with sighs,
...hing float her kisses meek,
...ies o'er my pallid cheek."

...ighing at his own tendency, but
...sitory thoughts of checking it.
...having left a Place of Retire-
...of dreaming,—

...f beds, pampering the coward heart
...gs all too delicate for use."

He is in revolt against the tendency, but only with his intellect. The honeysuckle intoxicates his heart too surely under the "indulgent skies" of that summer with Wordsworth.

A marked variety of his luxury is disclosed by his many references to the maiden's bosom and the swelling of it with emotion. I choose the following example because it includes so much that is characteristic besides,—

"Oft will I tell thee, Minstrel of the Moon,
'Most musical, most melancholy' Bird!
That all thy soft diversities of tune,
Tho' sweeter far than the delicious airs
That vibrate from a white-armed Lady's harp,
What time the languishment of lonely love
Melts in her eye, and heaves her breast of snow,

Are not so sweet as is the voice of her,
My Sara—best beloved of human kind !
When breathing the pure soul of tenderness,
She thrills me with the Husband's promised name ! "

This quality is more effective in company with
the other quality and relieved by it. I mean the
quality which responds to ghostliness and to the
wildness of Nature. " The Keepsake " has it
perfect, in this picture of a girl,—

" In the cool morning twilight, early waked
By her full bosom's joyous restlessness,
Softly she rose, and lightly stole along,
Down the slope coppice to the woodbine bower,
Whose rich flowers, swinging in the morning breeze,
Over their dim, fast-moving shadows hung,
Making a quiet image of disquiet
In the smooth, scarcely-moving river-pool."

It is perfect again, differently combined, in part of
" The Æolian Harp,"—

" The long sequacious notes
Over delicious surges sink and rise,
Such a soft floating witchery of sound
As twilight elfins make, when they at eve
Voyage on gentle gales from Fairy-Land,
Where Melodies round honey-dropping flowers,
Footless and wild, like birds of Paradise,
Nor pause, nor perch, hovering on untam'd wing ! "

The work of this best period, the Quantock

sojourn, shows this uniting of richness and delicacy, of sweetness and freshness, of sensuousness and wildness, of spirit and sense, irresistibly intruding on " Religious Musings," as here,—

> " When in some hour of solemn jubilee
> The massy gates of Paradise are thrown
> Wide open, and forth come in fragments wild
> Sweet echoes of unearthly melodies
> And odours snatched from beds of Amaranth,
> And they, that from the crystal river of life
> Spring up on freshened wing, ambrosial gales ; "

or, as in " Christabel " and " The Ancient Mariner," both written in the Quantocks, raised again and again to a peculiar harmony from the innermost parts of our poetry's holy of holies.

Except for Coleridge, I had the road to myself between ·Nether Stowey and Holford. Sheep were feeding on some of the slopes, and in one coomb woodmen were trimming cordwood among prostrate regiments of oak trees ; but these eaters of grass, or of bread and cheese and bacon, were ghosts by comparison with the man who wrote " The Ancient Mariner ; " the very hills, their chasms and processions of beeches, were made unforgettable by his May opium dream of—

> " That deep romantic chasm which slanted
> Down the green hill athwart a cedarn cover !

A savage place as holy and enchanted
As e'er beneath a waning moon was haunted
By woman wailing for her demon lover."

Then the sea. At a mile past Holford the road
bent sharp to the left and west, to get between the
sea and the Quantocks. A sign-board pointed to
the right to Stringston's red-roofed white church.
On the left two converging hillsides framed a wedge
of sea, divided into parallel bands of gray and blue.
It came as if it were a reward, an achievement, the
unsuspected aim of my meanderings. A long drift
of smoke lay over it from the seaward edge of the
hills. The bottom of the wedge held the village of
Kilve, and, a little apart, the cube of Kilve Court.
As if to a goal I raced downhill to Kilve and its
brook.

I had lunch at the " Hood Arms," and made up
my mind to stay there for that night. Two o'clock
had not long passed when I left the inn and the
main road and went north to Kilve Church and
the sea. The by-road accompanied the brook, and
skirted its apple orchards and tall poplars wagging
myriads of wine-red catkins. Having passed a mill,
a farm, and a cottage or two, the road took me to
the church and its big, short-boughed yew tree, and
became a farm track only. The small towered
church is a poor place, clean and newly repointed

outside, the arches filled in which had apparently communicated with a side chapel, and all its possible crosses lacking. Inside it has a cheap rickety gallery at the tower end, and was being stripped of its plaster to show the wood carving at the cornice. Tablets hang on the wall in memory of people named Cunditt and Sweeting, and of Norah Muriel Sweet-Escott, aged twenty, who died in South Africa of yellow fever. As I was leaving the church, entered the Other Man. Laughing nervously at the encounter, he explained that he had come to Kilve to see if it really had a weather-cock. He reminded me of Wordsworth's " Anecdote for Fathers," where the poet pesters his son of five to give his reason for preferring Liswyn to Kilve, until, a broad, gilded vane catching his eye, the child gives the inspired answer,—

> " At Kilve there is no weather-cock ;
> And that's the reason why."

" There *is* no weather-cock," said the Other Man, laughing a little more freely and disappearing for the last time. A white-fronted farm-house, the heavily ivy-mantled ruin of a chantry adjacent, green mounds of long submerged masonry, and a big knobby poplar with wine-red catkins, are next neighbours to the church, a stone's throw from the churchyard. The chantry has come to this by several stages. Part of it, for example, has been used as a dwelling, and adapted to the purpose by makeshift methods, which now add a sordid, contumelious element to the ruins. Fowls pecked about the chambers in the dust, in the bramble, ivy, and nettles. The big poplar stands, or, rather, reclines just off the ground, between the chantry and the brook. The running water led me seaward, through a tangled thicket of scrub oak, gorse, and bramble, filled in with teasel and burdock, and through a small marshy flag-bed. A low cliff, pierced by the stream, separates the beach from the rough, undulating, briery pasture. This cliff of sand and rock gave me shelter from the wind ; the flat gray pebbles gave me a seat ; and I looked out to sea.

A ragged sky hung threatening over a sea that was placid but corrugated and of the colour of slate, having a margin of black at the horizon. The water was hardly distinguishable, save by its motion, from the broad beach of gray pools, blackened pebbles, and low rock edges. Only the most fleeting and narrow lights fell upon the expanse, now on a solitary sail, now on the pale lighthouse of Flat Holm far out. Between this island, which just broke the surface of the sea on the left, and

Brean Down, the last outpost of the mainland
on the right, the cloudy pile of Steep Holm
towered up.

Not even the sea could altogether detain the eyes
from the land scene westward; for there massed
and jostled themselves together the main emi-
nences of Exmoor, of a uniform gray, soft and un-
moulded, that was lost from time to time either
in the wild, hurrying, and fitfully gleaming sky, or
in tawny smoke rolling low down from the Quantocks seaward.   Hardly less sublime was the long,
clear-cut ridge between me and Exmoor, low but
precipitous, projecting into the sea a mile or two
distant, and bearing a dark church tower like a
horn.   The fire on the Quantocks now burnt
scarlet.

The Kilve brook on my left was noisily twisting
over the pebbles and the slanting, gray, mossy-
weeded rock down to the sea, tossing up a light but
unceasing spray; and pied wagtails flitted from the
fresh water to the salt over the rocks.   But what I
was most glad to see was the meadow pipit. Feebly,
like a minor lark, and silently, he launched himself
twenty or thirty feet up from the wet, dark rock;
then, with wings uplifted and body curved to a
keel like a crescent, he descended slantwise, singing
the most passionate and thrilling-sweet of all songs

that " o'er inform this tenement of clay " until he
alighted. Before one had finished another began,
and not a moment was the song silenced. Here,
too, and among the briers of the rough pasture
behind the cliff, the wheatear, as clean as a star,
flirted his tail and showed his whiteness.

Over Exmoor storm and sun quarrelled in the
cauldron, but here only one drop fell on each dry,
warm pebble and vanished. The wind slackened ;
the heat grew; the warm, soft gray sky closed in
and imprisoned the air which the earth breathed.
It was pleasant to get hot out of doors in March. It
was pleasant to bicycle up out of Kilve and away
west on the Minehead road, which carried me well up
round the end of the Quantocks. I took the second
turning seaward for East Quantoxhead. The
cottage gardens in this lane were rich in wallflowers, daffodils, and jonquils ; and japonica was
blood-red on the walls. Still better were the hedges
past the few cottages, because they were green
entirely, and were the first I had seen so in that
spring. Nor were they mere thorn or elder
hedges, but interwoven elm, thorn, brier, and
elder, all with their young leaves expanded. But
the heat was already great, and I was going downhill too much not to reflect that I should have to
come up again. The pale Court House and con-

tiguous church of East Quantoxhead, homes of the living and of the dead Luttrells for many centuries, as men go, were still a quarter of a mile away across a wide meadow with oak trees, and I never got nearer. I turned instead along a hedged, stony lane upon the left. It soon created a suspicion that I ought not to have taken it. I stuck to it, however, uphill and then precipitously down under un-trimmed hedges, where it was no better than a river bed of mud and stones, until it ceased to exist, having emerged into the fields which it served. As I refused to return, I had to ascend along the edges of several ploughed fields and among sheepfolds and through gateways before I recovered the main road at about the sixth mile-stone from Nether Stowey. The heat, the climbing with a bicycle, and, above all, the useless, indignant impatience of annoyance, tired me; yet I rode on westward. The gorse was beautiful on the hills above, and in the old sandstone quarries beside the road. The sides of these quarries were bearded with it, their floors were carpeted with gilt moss, out of which rose up straight young larch trees in freshest green. At the head of a deep coomb of oak and foxglove the rock had been cut away for the widen-ing of the road, and from the newly exposed sand-stone hundreds of the rough rosettes of foxglove

had broken forth; but a smooth slab had been
devoted to an advertisement of somebody's flock
of long-woolled Devon sheep.

The approach to West Quantoxhead and the
great house of St. Audries was lined by fences,
and I rode down past them with dread of the
dismal walk back again. But at the foot the fence
came to an end. The pale gorsy turf of the deer
park fell away on the right to the great house and
its protecting woods. Daffodils and primroses were
thick on the left-hand slopes. And there was a
fountain of ever-running water at the roadside.
I took the water inwardly and outwardly, and no
longer troubled about the difficulty of ascent and
return, even when I found myself slipping down
hill for two miles into Williton. The high beacons
of Exmoor were hanging before me, scarfed and
coifed by clouds of the sunset, and grand were
these half-earthly and half-aerial heights, but lovelier
was the gentle hill much nearer and a little to the
left of my course. For the sun, sinking on the right
side of it, blessed and honoured this hill above all
other hills. Both its woods and pastures were burning subduedly with a mild orange fire, without being
consumed. It was the marriage of heaven and
earth. The grim beacons behind guarded the couch.
A white farm below was as white as moonlight.

Williton begins with a railway station and a workhouse; yet the first half mile of it is a street without a shop, of white or pale-washed, often thatched cottages and small houses, each separated from the road by flowery gardens of various breadths, some mere flowery strips, all good. To the fact that it was on the main road from Minehead to Bridgwater it was as indifferent as to the marriage of heaven and earth. The straight road was smooth, pale, and empty. Where it runs into another road, as the down stroke runs into the cross stroke of a T, and has a signpost to Watchet on the right, Bicknoller and Minehead on the left, the shops begin. Here, though it was six, and notwithstanding the marriage of heaven and earth, I had tea, and furthermore ate cream with a spoon, until I had had almost as much as I desired.

Now although I had seemed to be riding continually downhill into Williton, I found it nearly all downhill back to Kilve. The road was like a stream on which I floated in the shadows of trees and steep hillsides. The light was slowly departing, and still on some of the slopes the compact gorse bushes were like flocks of golden fleeces. Robins and blackbirds sang while bats were flitting about me. Day was not dead but sleeping, and the few stars overhead asked silence. By the turning to East Quantoxhead some cottagers talked in low tones. Kilve, dark and quiet, showed one or two faint lights. Only when I lay in bed did I recognize the two sounds that made the murmurous silence of Kilve—the whisper of its brook, and the bleat of sheep very far off.

19

X.

THE GRAVE OF WINTER.

W̱ I awoke at six the light was good, but it was the light of rain. One thrush alone was singing, a few starlings whistled. And the rain lasted until half-past eight. Then the sunlight enshrined itself in the room, the red road glistened, a Lombardy poplar at Kilve Court waved against a white sky only a little blemished by gray, and I started again westward. The black stain of yesterday's fire on the hill was very black, the new privet leaves very green, and the stitchwort very white in the arches of the drenched grass. The end of the rain, as I hoped, was sung away by missel-thrushes in the roadside oaks, by a chain of larks' songs which must have reached all over England.

I had some thoughts of branching off on one of the green lanes to the left, that would have led me past a thatched cottage or two up to the ridge of the Quantocks, to Stowborrow Hill, Beacon Hill, Thorncombe Hill, Great Hill, Will's Neck, Lydeard

Hill, Cothelstone Hill, and down to Taunton ; but
I kept to my road of last night as far as West Quantoxhead. There, beyond the fountain, I entered
the road between ranks of lime trees towards Stog-
umber. Before I had gone a mile the rain returned, and made the roads so bad that I had to
take to the highway from Williton to Taunton, and
so saw no more of Bicknoller than its brown tower.
But I had hopes of the weather, and the rain did no
harm to the flowers of periwinkle and laurustinus
in the hedges I was passing, and only added a sort
of mystery of inaccessibleness to the west wall of
the Quantocks, with which I was now going parallel.
It was a wall coloured in the main by ruddy dead
bracken and dark gorse, but patched sometimes
with cultivated strips and squares of green, and
trenched by deep coombs of oak, and by the shallow,
winding channels of streams—streams not of water
but of the most emerald grass. Seagulls mingled
with the rooks in the nearer fields. The only people
on the road were road-menders working with a
steam-roller ; the corduroys of one were stained so
thoroughly by the red mud of the Quantocks, and
shaped so excellently by wear to his tall, spare
figure, that they seemed to be one with the man.
It reminded me of " Lee Boo," and how the Pelew
Islanders doubted whether the clothes and bodies

of the white men did not " form one substance," and when one took off his hat they were struck with astonishment, " as if they thought it had formed part of his head."

The rain ceased just soon enough not to prove again the vanity of waterproofs. I have, it is true, discovered several which have brought me through a storm dry in parts, but I have also discovered that sellers of waterproofs are among the worst of liars, and that they communicate their vice with their goods. The one certain fact is that nobody makes a garment or suit which will keep a man both dry and comfortable if he is walking in heavy and beating rain. Suits of armour have, of course, been devised to resist rain, but at best they admit it at the neck. The ordinary (and extraordinary) waterproof may keep a man dry from neck to groin, though it is improbable exceedingly that both neck and wrists will escape. As for the legs, the rain gets at the whole of them with the aid of wind and capillary attraction. Whoever wore a coat that kept his knees dry in a beating rain ? I am not speaking of waterproof tubes reaching to the feet. They may be sold, they may even be bought. They may be useful, but not for walking in.

For moderate showers one waterproof is about

as good as another. The most advertised have the advantage of being expensive, and conferring distinction otherwise : they are no better, and wear worse, than a thing at two-thirds of the price which is never advertised at all. In such a one I was riding now, and I got wet only at the ankles. It actually kept my knees dry in the heavy rain near Timsbury. But if I had been walking I should have been intolerably hot and embarrassed in this, and very little less so in the lighter, more distinguished, more expensive garment. Supposing that a thorough waterproof exists, so light as to be comfortable in mild weather, it is certain to have the grave disadvantage of being easily tearable, and therefore of barring the wearer from woods.

Getting the body wet even in cold weather is delicious, but getting clothes and parts of the body wet, especially about and below the knee, is detestable. Trousers, and still more breeches, when wet through, prove unfriendly to man, and in some degree to boy. If the knees were free and the feet bare, I should think there would be no impediment left to bliss for an active man in shower or storm, except that he would provoke, evoke, and convoke laughter, and ninety-nine out of a hundred would prefer to this all the evils of rain and of waterproofs. It is to save our clothes and to lessen the discomfort of them that a waterproof is added.

At first thought, it is humiliating to realize that we have spent many centuries in this climate and never produced anything to keep us dry and comfortable in rain. But who are we that complain? Not farmers, labourers, and fishermen, but people who spend much time out of doors by choice. We can go indoors when it rains; only, we do not wish to, because so many of the works of rain are good—in the skies, on the earth, in the souls of men and also of birds. When youth is over we are not carried away by our happiness so far as to ignore soaked boots and trousers. We like hassocks to kneel on, and on those hassocks we pray for a waterproof. As the prayer is only about a hundred years old—a hundred years ago there were no such beings—it is not surprising that the answer has not arrived from that distant quarter. Real outdoor people have either to do without waterproofs, or what they use would disable us from our pleasures. Naturally, they have done nothing to solve our difficulties. They have not written poetry for us, they have not made waterproofs for us. They do not read our poetry, they do not wear our waterproofs. We must solve the question by complaint and experiment, or by learning to go wet—an increasingly hard lesson for a generation that multiplies conveniences and inconveniences rather faster than it does an honest love of sun, wind, and rain, separately and all together.

By the time I reached Crowcombe, the sun was bright. This village, standing at the entrance to a great cloudy coomb of oaks and pine trees, is a thatched street containing the " Carew Arms," a long, white inn having a small porch, and over it a signboard bearing a coat of arms and the words " *J'espère bien.*" The street ends in a cross, a tall, slender, tapering cross of stone, iron-brown and silver-spotted. Here also sang a chiffchaff, like a clock rapidly ticking. The church is a little beyond, near the rookery of Crowcombe Court. Its red tower on the verge of the high roadside bank is set at the north-west corner in such a way—perhaps it is not quite at right angles—that I looked again and again up to it, as at a man in a million.

After passing Flaxpool, a tiny cluster of dwellings and ricks, with a rough, rising orchard, then a new-made road with a new signpost to Bridgwater, and then a thatched white inn called the " Stag's Head," I turned off for West Bagborough, setting my face toward the wooded flank of Bagborough Hill. Bagborough Church and Bagborough House stand at the edge of the wood. The village houses either touch the edge of the road, or, where it is very steep, lie back behind walls which were hanging their white and purple clouds of alyssum and aubretia down to the wayside water. Rain threatened again, and I went into the inn to eat and see what would happen. Two old men sat in the small settle at the fireside talking of the cold weather, for so they deemed it. Bent, grinning, old men they were, using rustic, deliberate, grave speech, as they drank their beer and ate a few fancy biscuits. One of them was so old that never in his life had he done a stroke of gardening on a Good Friday; he knew a woman that did so once when he was a lad, and she perished shortly after in great pain. His own wife, even now, was on her death-bed; she had eaten nothing for weeks, and was bad-tempered, though still sensible. But when the rain at last struck the window like a swarm of bees, and the wind drove the smoke out into the room, the old man was glad to be where he was, not out of doors or up in the death room. His talk was mostly of the weather, and his beans, and his peas, which he was so pleased with that he was going to send over half a pint of them to the other old man. The biscuits they were eating set him thinking of better biscuits. For example, now, a certain kind made formerly at Watchet was very

good. But the best of all were Half Moon biscuits.
They had a few caraways in them, which they did
not fear, because, old as they were, they were not
likely to have leisure for appendicitis. Half a one
in your cup of tea in the morning would *plim out*
and fill the cup. They told me the street, the side
of the street, the shop, its neighbours on either
side, in Taunton, where I might hope to buy Half
Moon biscuits even in the twentieth century. The
whitening sky and the drops making the window
pane dazzle manifested the storm's end, and the
old men thought of the stag hounds, which were
to meet that day. . . . Just above Bagborough
there, seven red stags had been seen, not so long
ago.

It was hot again at last as I climbed away from
the valley and its gently sloping green and rosy
squares and elmy hedges, up between high, loose
banks of elder and brier, and much tall arum,
nettle, and celandine, and one plant of honesty
from the last cottage garden. High as it was, the
larch coppice on the left far up had a chiffchaff
singing in it, and honeysuckle still interwove
itself in the gorse and holly of the roadside. A
parallel, deep-worn, green track mounted the hill,
close on my right, and there was a small square
ruin covered with ivy above it among pine trees. It

was not the last building. A hundred feet up, in a slight dip, I came to a farm-house, Tilbury Farm. Both sides of the road there are lined by mossy banks and ash and beech trees, and deep below, southward, on the right hand, I saw through the trees the gray mass of Cothelstone Manor-house beside its lake, and twelve miles off in the same direction the Wellington obelisk on the Black Down Hills. A stone seat on the other side of the trees commands both the manor house beneath and the distant obelisk. The seat is in an arched-over recess in the thickness of a square wall of masonry, six or seven feet in height and breadth. A coeval old hawthorn, spare and solitary, sticks out from the base of the wall. The whole is surmounted by a classic stone statue of an emasculated man larger than human, nude except for some drapery falling behind, long-haired, with left arm uplifted, and under its feet a dog; and it looks straight over at the obelisk. I do not know if the statue and the obelisk are connected, nor, if so, whether the statue represents the Iron Duke, his king, or a classic deity; the mutilation is against the last possibility. Had the obelisk not been so plainly opposite, I should have taken the figure for some sort of a god, the ponderous, rustic-classic fancy of a former early nineteenth-century owner of Cothelstone

Manor. The statue and masonry, darkened and bitten by weather, in that high, remote, commanding place, has in any case long outgrown the original conception and intention, and become a classi-rustical, romantic what-you-please, waiting for its poet or prose poet. I should have liked very well, on such a day, in such a position, to think it a Somerset Pan or Apollo, but could not. It was mainly pathetic and partly ridiculous. In the mossy bank behind it the first woodsorrel flower drooped its white face among primroses and green moschatel knobs; they made the statue, lacking ivy and moss, seem harsh and crude. Some way farther on, where the beeches on that hand come to an end, two high stout pillars, composed of alternate larger and smaller layers of masonry, stand gateless and as purposeless as the king, duke, or god.

For a while I rested in a thatched shed at the summit, 997 feet up, where the road turns at right angles and makes use of the ridge track of the Quantocks. A roller made of a fir trunk gave me a seat, and I looked down this piece of road, which is lined by uncommonly bushy beeches, and over at Cothelstone Hill, a dome of green and ruddy grasses in the south-east, sprinkled with thorn trees and capped by the blunt tower of a beacon. The primrose roots hard by me had each sufficient flowers to make a child's handful.

Turning to the left again, when the signpost declared it seven and three-quarter miles to Bridgwater, I found myself on a glorious sunlit road without hedge, bank, or fence on either side, proceeding through fern, gorse, and ash trees scattered over mossy slopes. Down the slopes I looked across the flat valley to the Mendips and Brent Knoll, and to the Steep and Flat Holms, resting like clouds on a pale, cloudy sea ; what is more, through a low-arched rainbow I saw the blueness of the hills of South Wales. The sun had both dried the turf and warmed it. The million gorse petals seemed to be flames sown by the sun. By the side of the road were the first bluebells and cowslips. They were not growing there, but some child had gathered them below at Stowey or Durleigh, and then, getting tired of them, had dropped them. They were beginning to wilt, but they lay upon the grave of Winter. I was quite sure of that. Winter may rise up through mould alive with violets and primroses and daffodils, but when cowslips and bluebells have grown over his grave he cannot rise again : he is dead and rotten, and from his ashes the blossoms are springing. Therefore, I was very glad to see them. Even to have seen them on a railway station seat in the rain, brought from far off on an Easter Monday, would have been something; here, in the sun, they were as if they had been fragments fallen out of that rainbow over against Wales. I had found Winter's grave; I had found Spring, and I was confident that I could ride home again and find Spring all along the road. Perhaps I should hear the cuckoo by the time I was again at the Avon, and see cowslips tall on ditchsides and short on chalk slopes, bluebells in all hazel copses, orchises everywhere in the lengthening grass, and flowers of rosemary and crown-imperial in cottage gardens, and in the streets of London cowslips, bluebells, and the unflower-like yellow-green spurge. . . . Thus I leapt over April and into May, as I sat in the sun on the north side of Cothelstone Hill on that 28th day of March, the last day of my journey westward to find the Spring.

THE END.

Printed in the United Kingdom by
Lightning Source UK Ltd., Milton Keynes
142370UK00001B/214/A